A

CANDLELIGHT REGENCY SPECIAL

CANDLELIGHT REGENCIES

A WORTHY CHARADE

Vivian Harris

A CANDLELIGHT REGENCY SPECIAL

Published by
Dell Publishing Co., Inc.
1 Dag Hammarskjold Plaza
New York, New York 10017

Dell ® TM 681510, Dell Publishing Co., Inc.

ISBN: 0-440-14378-0

Printed in the United States of America
First printing—October 1980

Chapter I

"Where's Sissy?" Katherine asked as she smoothed the soft gray glove onto her hand. "I thought surely she would be ready in plenty of time."

"And that she was, milady. She's already in the coach, as impatient to be on her way as a gypsy with a stolen hen."

Katherine nodded, a slight smile twisting her lips. "I'm not at all surprised." Then, turning to the motherly woman standing by her side, a look of concern darkened her lovely gray eyes. "And you, Mrs. Grimsly, are you sure everything will be all right here while I'm away?"

Mrs. Grimsly, a big-boned woman well-advanced in years, stiffened and with haughty dignity replied, "I can take care of the house. Haven't I been doing just that for nigh on to twenty years already? And Samson is quite capable of managing the farm." She paused, her eyes lighting up with affection, and her tone softened. "Now don't you worry about anything. Nothing can go wrong. You just see to it that Gwen has the time of her life . . . and it seems to me that you should enjoy yourself a bit too. You certainly haven't—"

"Oh, please, don't start on that again," Katherine interrupted good-naturedly. "You know well enough there's no place I'd rather be than right here at Blue Hills."

"But—"

"No more," Katherine admonished gently. "Besides, I must leave now before Sissy is cast into a quake."

For a second more Katherine rested her hand on the older woman's arm, and then impulsively she reached over and kissed her wrinkled cheek. Turning quickly, Katherine went out, giving a quick affectionate good-bye to the butler, who had been holding the door open, patiently awaiting her departure.

Mrs. Grimsly and the butler were joined by several other servants as they followed Katherine down the stone stairs to the waiting coach. An aged but alert and spry groom sprang forward to assist her up the steps into the carriage. Shutting the door behind her, the groom leaped up to his seat beside the driver, motioned to the two outriders, and the coach lumbered forward.

After waving a final adieu to her faithful well-wishers, Katherine settled back to a more comfortable position, never taking her eyes from the huge rambling building that seemed to blend harmoniously with the shrubs and trees that surrounded it. The blue haze of the hills, rising protectively behind, spread over the entire scene, until the soft hue was all that Katherine could see as the powerful horses galloped on, carrying them away.

The reverent silence was broken by the young miss seated across from Katherine. "'Tis beautiful," she whispered.

"Yes, Sissy, it is and it's home," agreed Katherine with the same breathless awe in her tone.

But for how long? Katherine questioned herself. Closing her eyes, she pictured the large bright rooms, the long narrow windows with the rich heavy drapes pulled back to allow the sun's rays an easy access to the most distant corner. True, she had been born here, had spent all of the almost twenty-three years of her life beneath its roof, had buried her parents in the small chapel graveyard, and had assumed the responsibilities of caring for her younger siblings. But one day she would have to leave. She was only holding it in trust for the fifth earl.

The pictures in her mind swiftly changed to the fine chiseled features of a fair young boy, his curly hair unkempt, his blue eyes bright with interest, his mouth curved in a slight, pleasing smile. She remembered him as he was when he had returned home from school during the last holiday. She was sure he had grown two inches during that short term. In a little over four years Blue Hills would legally be his alone. He was sixteen, now, nearly seventeen. Soon he'd be bringing a wife to be mistress of the only home she had ever known.

"Why, milady, is ought amiss?" Sissy's concerned voice broke into Katherine's reflections.

"No, no, Sissy. I just hate leaving Blue Hills even for a short time."

"But, milady, we're going to London."

Katherine sighed. "Yes, Sissy, London," she said, but her voice echoed none of her companion's excited anticipation.

"Anyway, we'll be with Miss Gwen," Sissy continued, attempting to bolster Katherine's spirits.

Katherine smiled as she surveyed the young girl. "This is quite a treat for you, isn't it, Sissy?"

"La, milady, you know it. When me ma told me you wanted me—me, Sissy Colpepper—to be your maid and to go with you to the city, I didn't believe her. I couldn't believe her." Sissy's eyes grew wider and rounder as she spoke. "I still think I'll waken and find it all a dream."

Laughing, Katherine answered, "It is no dream, Sissy. You are definitely my maid and we are on our way to London."

Though Sissy was really too young, barely in her teens, and totally inexperienced, Katherine had felt there was no one else in the household that could be released from her duties for the time needed for this journey. She had had some apprehensions about requesting Sissy's presence, but after seeing the elation the assignment had given the child, Katherine had easily tossed all her doubts aside.

The journey proceeded without incident as the carriage rumbled over many miles of the Devon countryside, and entered Dorset. The weather, warm for early spring, was bright at times and misty at others, but in no way impeded their progress. During the late afternoon though the sun assimilated the heat of midsummer, turning the old-fashioned coach into an uncomfortable box of heated humidity. Its occupants, already fatigued, their every muscle aching from the constant jostling, were now forced to endure the added discomfort of the stifling heat.

Finally Katherine opened the panel at the front of the coach and called to the coachman, "Sommers, for mercy's sake, if there is even a remotely respectable inn in the next village, let us stop for a few minutes. We're being cooked to a turn in here."

"Yes, Miss Katherine, will do. The horses could use a bit of a breather too."

A short time later Katherine and Sissy, heaving sighs of relief, stepped down from the coach at the entrance of a very modern, brightly painted hostelry, remarkably large for the village of which it was a part.

"It seems, milady, that this here road is more and more in use," the groom remarked as he noted Katherine's look of surprise at the sight of the imposing building. "There's several of these new establishments being built along its way."

"I must say it's mighty impressive. Better than I had hoped for," she returned.

Entering the inn, Katherine was pleased at the large common room, clean and bright, furnished with a number of small tables, which for the most part were presently unoccupied. She refused the innkeeper's offer of a private parlor, saying that they were only stopping long enough to refresh themselves with something cool to drink.

Nodding in understanding, the innkeeper led them to one of the tables near a large bay window and motioned to a serving maid. Katherine was a bit relieved to note that seated at one of the other tables were three unescorted, well-dressed females and at another two gentlemen clothed in the finest toggery Katherine had seen in many a day. Truly this was a respectable inn.

After giving their order of lemonade and biscuits, Katherine and Sissy sat back in the comfortable chairs and smiled at each other as their eyes met. Sissy stole a furtive glance at the two gentlemen, biting her lip to keep from giggling.

"I ain't seen nothin' like them before, milady," she said with difficulty as she tried to keep a straight face.

"You had better get used to it, my dear. You'll be seeing a number of the dandy set mincing their way down the London streets."

"You mean they dress like that in London?"

"Some do."

"Oh, milady, this is all so strange, so exciting—"

"Sissy, you make me feel like a tired old woman," Katherine answered with a laugh.

"Not you, milady." Sissy smiled, her disbelief echoed in her eyes.

The serving wench brought their lemonade and a plate piled high with all manner of freshly baked tarts, and with unladylike haste the two proceeded to quench their thirsts and enjoy the delicacies.

A hearty, derisive laugh directed Katherine's attention toward the two gentlemen who had been the subject of their amusement minutes before.

"That estate, my dear man, around here is called Milford's Madness." The gentleman's tone was as scornful as his laugh.

"Madness? Why, it looks to be a delightful manor," his companion stated.

"Oh, that it was, before Milford won it at a turn of

the card. But after taking possession, he turned it into a school."

"A school. What's mad about that? Such a venture properly run can be quite advantageous."

"Quite true," agreed the first man, "but not this one. Its sole purpose is to educate the farm children and the pauper urchins from the cities. It certainly doesn't bring in any blunt. As I hear it, it has been a drain on Milford's sources. He spends most of his time trying to persuade his acquaintances to reach into their pockets or, worse yet, he's trying to push through laws that would support these young whelps with government money."

"Really?" interposed the second. "Ridiculous. I see what you mean by madness."

Scorn scorching his words, the first gentleman continued, "Milford's trying to set up another one to the north. He may have a fortune, but he'll soon find himself in the suds if he continues on with these hair-brained schemes. What a stupid waste."

Katherine took a more speculative note of the two men as she listened to their conversation. A few of the guineas spent on their foolish fobs and fine clothes donated instead to education—no matter whose—would certainly have been much less a waste. But there was something else that had caught her attention in their conversation—the name Milford. Had she heard it before? She strained her memory but could not come up with an answer.

Her interest in her fellow travelers was short-lived, as Sissy had finished her repast and began to question her again on the delights of London. Atfer answering a couple of questions to the best of her knowledge, which was not overly great since Katherine herself had been to the city only a few times, she laughed and admonished her companion.

"Hush, Sissy, in a few hours you will be there yourself, and if we want to arrive before dark we had better be on our way."

Chapter II

The door opened, revealing Dame Martha's slight, straight form, her white hair piled high on her head to add inches to her diminutive figure. But it was the way she held her head, the graceful movements of her arms and hands that gave her the dignity she exemplified.

"Gerry." An affectionate smile brightened her face. "It's good to see you." She greeted the young man who was seated in an overstuffed chair, glancing idly through a copy of the *London Chronicle*.

Immediately the young man jumped to his feet and in two long strides was before her, grasping her extended hands in his.

"There's no need to ask how you are, Grandmama. You look marvelous as usual," he said fondly, surveying her from tip to toe.

"And you also seem to be enjoying good health."

"No complaints."

As the two exchanged their salutatory comments, the young man led his grandmother to a large wing-backed chair, which he moved a little closer to the one he had just vacated.

"And how are things at Milford Hall?" Dame Martha continued after seating herself in the proffered chair.

"Fine, exceptionally fine, especially since Pamela and her two offspring have finally settled in. Those two young ones do add life to the place," her grandson responded.

For a moment Dame Martha was silent, her lips twisted into a tiny smile, a faraway look in her eyes, as if she might be remembering the happy sounds of children at play.

"They are a twosome, aren't they?" Then a sterner note crept into her voice. "When did you arrive in town, Gerald? No one even mentioned the fact that you were around."

Chuckling, Gerry answered, "You still have your cronies keeping you up to date. Well, I doubt as if any of them would have seen me this time. I've only been here two days and both have been spent almost entirely on business."

"I see," Dame Martha commented dryly. Since her grandson didn't add any more information, she inquired rather stringently, "Any particular reason for your call this afternoon?"

"Why, my dear madam, isn't just my wish to see you again reason enough?" he countered teasingly.

"Poof! I'd be delighted if that were the case, but I know you have at least two reasons for everything you do."

"Truthfully, this time I would say my desire to see you was the prime one, for I am in need of a little bolstering. I'm becoming a little disgusted with my peers and need a lecture on patience and understanding." The pleasantness had left his voice, and his tone indicated a decided weariness of spirit.

"Am I to deduce from what you said before and

that dejected statement that your business was in Parliament and that your enlightened proposals have met with the usual coldness?" Though Dame Martha kept her voice light, there was a sincere look of concern upon her face.

"Coldness? How about absolute frigidity?" was his abrupt answer.

"I'm truly sorry about that, Gerry. You must know that many do not view your schemes as a boon to the country but as a definite force for the destruction of their own powers. It soothes their consciences to pay out a few shillings to feed and clothe the poor, but to arm them with education instills some with absolute fear."

"Hmmp," Gerry snorted. "I heard some of their reasoning today. They equate ruling with grinding people under their heels."

Dame Martha shrugged. "Possibly you are right. It's a sorry comment. Were you entirely unsuccessful?"

"No, not entirely. I felt I was able to convince a few minds at least to consider my project. It's a shame Lady Haverly doesn't hold a seat instead of that ninnie she married."

"Lord Haverly's not against you, surely?"

"No, not against me but he's no help. His snores don't hold the weight of the barbed phrases his wife could come up with."

Gerry sat musing for a few moments, then looked up again at his grandmother. "You know, Grandmama," he exclaimed in extreme seriousness, "I am going to have to get married."

Dame Martha's eyes widened in shocked surprise. "Married? Really, Gerry, after all I've done to induce you to take that step, what has finally brought you around? I don't see any connection between your marriage and your schools."

"But there is a connection, a definite connection." Gerry rubbed his chin reflectively. "Who are my biggest backers, not counting Lord Russell himself? Lady Haverly, Lady Beardsly, Miss Snettering—all women. How many more enlightened females who hold the purse strings or are capable of influencing their husbands are there that I've no way of contacting? So far, I've fought my battles on the floor, at Whites, at the coffee houses. But I'm losing. If I were able to entertain properly, hold informal dinners that would include the wives—carefully selecting the influential—I might make more headway."

Still perplexed, Dame Martha remarked, "I still don't see what that has to do with getting married."

"Everything! I need the proper hostess. I can't conduct this type of dinner in bachelor quarters. I need a lovely young bride to put the gentlemen at ease, one who is sincere, agreeable, and amiable and who can smooth the way as far as the ladies are concerned."

"Really, Gerald," Dame Martha gasped, incredulity straining her voice. "I've never heard of anything so ridiculous."

"Ridiculous? Why?" Gerry stiffened; his voice became harsh. "You've been badgering me ever since I sold out to take on a wife. Now that I've decided to do so, you call me ridiculous."

"But to marry just to procure a hostess?"

"Madam, is that any less a reason for marriage than to hold on to a house?"

At these words the color heightened in Dame Martha's cheeks. "You're being exasperating. You know there's a great deal more involved in marrying to produce an heir than to just holding on to a house."

With a sudden laugh, Gerry relaxed. "I'm sorry, Grandmama. You're right, of course. I've just met with enough obstacles today to—still that doesn't give me the right to lash out at you. Forgive me."

"Of course, Gerry, I understand."

"Anyway why are we at odds?" he continued in a conciliatory tone. "What does my reason for marrying matter? We'll both be getting what we want."

"I do hope so. . . ." Her voice faded. Then, with a sudden brightness as if to push away unwanted ideas, Dame Martha gazed at her grandson, a teasing glint in her eyes. "Who do you intend to choose? Lady Sophia?"

"Good God, no! No reigning, spoiled beauty. No, I've picked out a very sweet, completely charming country miss." Seeing the frown that again began to crease Dame Martha's forehead, he hastened to add, "Of impeccable breeding from a respectable family. Qualities that are a must for my hostess, you realize."

"Do I know her?"

"As a matter of fact, madam, I think you did meet her once or twice and were quite impressed. I became acquainted with her while visiting you in Bath late last summer."

"Tell me, Gerry. Stop your teasing. Who is she?"

"Do you remember a Miss Tarkington? Gwen Tarkington?"

Dame Martha remained silent for a time. Then a

look of recognition flashed in her eyes. "That delightful child!"

"An apt description. I stood up with her for a couple of dances at the assembly and we enjoyed some conversation. I found her to be, besides extremely lovely to behold, quite refreshing to be with."

"You don't think she's too young for you?" There was hesitancy in Dame Martha's voice as she peered at her grandson.

Gerald shrugged indifferently. "There is an age difference, I will admit, but I'm not yet considering the grave." He gave his grandmother a wide, mischievous grin. "In fact, being with her makes me feel quite a few years younger."

"You've seen her recently?"

"Yes, I have. Just last night. I dropped in at Lady Beardsly's musical. Why didn't you attend?"

"Matilda gave a dinner in honor of Matt's coming of age. I was bespoken for."

"Really. In any case we renewed our acquaintance there and—"

"That's when you came up with the idea that you needed a hostess." Dame Martha's chuckling finished for him.

"Something like that," he admitted.

Leaning forward in her chair, as if reaching out to her grandson, Dame Martha asked in a husky voice, "Are you in love with her, Gerry?"

"Love," he repeated. The merry twinkle left his eyes and he looked at her solemnly. "No, Grandmama, not the way you mean. I'm no romantic and have very little faith in the grand passion. Miss Tarkington is charming, delightful, and very beautiful. We'll do well together, I'm sure."

As if disappointed by the matter-of-factness of his tone, Dame Martha leaned back again in her chair and sighed. "I'm truly sorry. I had hoped that you might marry for love as your father did."

A bitter laugh was her immediate answer. "And what did that achieve for him—an early grave."

"But he did have a number of years of happiness."

"I suppose so, but I don't remember them . . . only poverty and sickness. No, his marriage is not an example to be holding before me as one blessed, nor was yours, Grandmama," he said, looking fondly at her.

The two sat in companionable silence, the Lord Gerald Milton Rutherford Milford, Earl of Sandwell, quietly studying the aging face of the woman sitting next to him. How much he owed to her. She alone had confronted his grandfather, continuing to accept his parents after they had been ostracized from family and society. In open defiance of her husband she had seen to it that after his parents died he had all the advantages of his class. Yes, it was a good thing that he had finally decided to marry. He had always known how much she wanted to see the line continue—how much she wanted Milford Hall to remain in the family.

And as if reading his thoughts, Dame Martha sighed. "Anyway, Francis won't get his hands on Milford Hall now."

A teasing light danced in Gerry's eyes as he grinned at her. "We'll have a hostess and a house, eh, Grandmama?"

Chapter III

The first sights of London stirred no appreciation within Katherine. She had known they wouldn't. In fact they evoked bitter memories . . . memories of bewilderment, humiliation, and, finally, disgust.

Five years had passed and, though she had returned several times to attend to necessary business matters for the estate and to shop for items unattainable in Brighton or Exeter, taking the opera and theater as pleasant diversions, she never remained longer than required. As far as Katherine was concerned, those first few miserable weeks of her coming out had been more than enough of the highly touted social life she found so distasteful.

Sitting back and resting her head against the rich velvet of the carriage cushions, she couldn't block out those heartbreaking recollections that still occasionally forced themselves upon her. She recalled how eagerly she had prepared for her presentation, how her mother had nurtured her on the gaiety, the pleasures, the balls, the handsome swains.

Unfortunately, in remembering her own glorious debut, Katherine's mother had not taken into account the vast differences between herself and her oldest daughter. Loving her and knowing her for the warm-hearted, intelligent girl she was, Katherine's mother had been blinded to the dissimilarities that the members of society—the ton—were sure to pounce upon. Whereas Lady Alicia had been a talented beauty, Katherine was plain, even gawky. Tall and undeveloped for her age, Katherine's figure resembled, to put it bluntly, a bean pole. Lady Alicia had been reared in a family entrenched in society, had learned the art of casual, witty conversation, even of coquettery, and had thrived on it. Katherine, on the other hand, spending her entire life riding alongside her father among the blue-green hills of Devon, had grown into a physically active though shy young miss. She was at ease seated on a horse in the wide open fields, thoroughly happy engrossed in the care of a sick lamb or a newly foaled calf, but was practically suffocated by the press of people within the enclosure of four walls.

So it was not surprising to one knowledgeable in the ways of the ton that, left to her own devices, the young Katherine's debut was far from a success. Shortly before her departure for London, Lady Alicia was taken to her bed, but she would not tolerate the thought of her first daughter being denied the opportunity to meet the world she had so loved in her own youth. She insisted that Katherine stay with a distant relative, who was also bringing out her own daughter that year.

Unfortunately Cousin Rachael's daughter was as unendowed as Katherine, and though Rachael had no objection in chaperoning her young relative, she had no time to see to it that she mingled with the right people or came to the notice of available young gentlemen. After all, a mother must take care of her own, and in the case of Rachael's daughter, that was a time-consuming task.

Though Katherine's gowns were as elegant, as taste-fully cut, and as fashionable as any others, they hung unflatteringly on her straight lean frame. In the country she had never bothered to style her soft curly brown hair. She had not the time to waste—besides, the horses and farm animals with whom she spent most of her days didn't care. The young maid provided by Cousin Rachael, though willing, was entirely unimaginative, even inept.

Katherine was certainly noticed. Inches taller than any of the other young females, she could not be missed. But the eyes of kinder souls quickly passed over her so as not to embarrass her by building up the eager expectations that showed so plainly in her face. Those more insensitive looked her over boldly and, with a smirk, made some disparaging remark to their companions.

After her first humiliating ball, Katherine faced the next parties with fading hopes but grim determination. She was proud and intelligent. She knew she could seat a horse and dance better than anyone who moved around the floor. But she soon realized that she would never be allowed to prove her capabilities. She couldn't race a horse across the ballroom floor. Nor could she display her natural grace in the dance if only a few shy, awkward lads stood up with her.

After two weeks of disappointment and disillusionment, she received word that her mother had become increasingly ill. Katherine left London, her grief solely caused by the shadow that hung over her dear mother and not one bit by her sudden departure from the festivities of the city.

The next three years had been difficult ones for the maturing, young Katherine. She had arrived home in time to make the arrangements for her mother's funeral and was then immediately thrust into the responsibilities of an almost impossible position. Her father, bereft by the loss of his beloved wife, seemed to care less and less about the lives of those around him, and Katherine was forced to assume not only the role of mistress of Blue Hills and the sole charge of her two younger sisters and brother, but the management of the huge estate as well.

It was her nature to accept what came without complaint and to apply all her energies to the matter at hand. So capable did she become that the steward was soon seeking her out for consultations and instructions, bypassing her father who would have probably told him to seek her advice anyway. She became a familiar figure in Brighton and Exeter as she accompanied her father on all matters of business, and her knowledge and shrewdness soon made her an acceptable equal among the wealthy landowners of the area. It came as no surprise to them that, when her father died just a scant three years after his wife, he had bestowed complete control of the estate and her younger siblings to Katherine, until young Clifford would be of age to take his rightful place.

Managing the estate was no small task, but by this time Katherine had grown accustomed to the many demands, and she thrived on the challenge. As she had increased her knowledge of management, she had also cultivated her social graces, quickly learning the necessary art of trivial conversation as well as meaningful dialogue. She became equally at home in the dining halls, salons, and cluttered offices as she had been in the barns and open fields. No longer was she a thin, shapeless nonentity; she had been transformed into a beautiful woman now endowed with a full, well-rounded figure with added height that gave her dignity and a natural grace that cloaked her every movement with a royal elegance.

The young men of her acquaintance held her in admiration and awe, but they were fully aware that they were not up to coping with her independence. Older men, whose wives had died or who had not had the opportunity or inclination to marry, sought her affections, but they left her unmoved. She would rather be her own champion than depend on has-beens or inadequates.

Now, at twenty-three, she was again entering the social life in London, though not by choice. She had no desire to tear herself away from the beauties of Devon and the business of the estate to chase from party to party in dirty, noisy, hostile London. But again she felt that her responsibility lay in that direction and she would acquiesce.

This was the season for Gwen, her lovely younger sister, and as much as she did not desire that task, when Gwen wrote begging her to act as her chaperon, she felt she had to oblige. Lady Metcalf, a dear friend of their mother's, had eagerly accepted Gwen's sponsorship but had had an accident and would not be physically able to escort her to the many activities planned for the rest of the season. The lot now fell to Katherine.

From Gwen's first excited letters Katherine realized that her sister's coming out was in sharp contrast to her own. A replica of her mother, Gwen had accomplished a triumphant beginning under the guidance of the astute and knowledgeable Lady Metcalf. The pattern had already been set. Gwen had been besieged by eager young hopefuls and her activities scheduled for weeks in advance. Although fate had intervened and Lady Metcalf was no longer able to take an active part, Katherine would be a perfect replacement.

So here she was again about to enter the life that had once filled her with humiliation and despair, but this time she sighed gratefully, only as a chaperon.

As the curricle made its way slowly across Westminster Bridge and into the city streets, the noise of vendors hawking their wares, the newsboys with their horns, the scavengers with their handbells, and even the wail of the ballad singers seemed to lift Katherine's spirits. Her maid's undeniable excitement became contagious.

Had she been too frightened the first time to sense the excitement about her? Too bitter on her few other visits? Though Katherine realized the mobs and the din were the same, for some reason they appeared different . . . or was it she who had changed?

Katherine pointed out a few of the places of interest with which she was familiar as her maid bobbed from one window to another.

"Sissy, we'll be here for some time. Relax," Katherine said, laughing, in no way disturbed by the unmannered activity of the enthralled girl.

"I'm sorry, milady, I'll—" The young lass bent her

head, clasping her hands together tightly in an effort to compose herself.

The effort was almost immediately abandoned as their coach labored up the magnificent road from Charing Cross to White Chapel and Katherine again began to point out the shops where she had purchased a few items.

As they traveled on to less crowded thoroughfares, their pace quickened. Katherine knew how capable Sommers was, and felt no apprehension. She was eager to put an end to their long, tedious journey. But when Sommers braked the coach to a sudden stop in front of Lady Metcalf's town house with an abruptness that threw her from her seat, Katherine was ready to give him a good dressing down that would make him more aware of the need for care in city driving. Frowning, she settled back into her seat, but instead of Sommers coming to open the door and letting down the stairs, she heard him mutter an oath—or was it a prayer?—as he scrambled down from his perch and headed for the lead horse. Impatient, Katherine opened the door and stretched out her head to determine what had delayed her groom. She caught sight of billowing skirts lying just in front of the nervous horses' hooves. Not waiting for assistance, she gathered her skirts to the side, jumped to the ground, and hurried to join Sommers. There on the ground, just inches from possible death, lay an unconscious young woman.

"Milady, she stepped right out in front of me," cried Sommers. "I couldn't stop any quicker. Oh, God, she isn't dead?" His sincere anguish was evident in his lined face and fervent tone.

Quickly Katherine knelt beside the woman. "No, Sommers, she's alive, but I can't tell how badly she's hurt."

By that time the door to Lady Metcalf's had opened and the butler and young manservant were racing down the steps.

Rising, Katherine greeted them calmly. "I'm afraid there's been an accident, Reynolds. I'm Katherine Tarkington. You may not remember me, but I am sure I am expected. For now, would you see that this young woman is taken to the room prepared for me? Be careful, she may be seriously injured."

As the young woman in question was small, Sommers had no difficulty in carrying her, once she had been lifted into his arms, and he followed the young manservant into the house, Katherine and the butler directly behind them.

"Tell Lady Metcalf and my sister that I am here and please offer my apologies for not greeting them myself upon my arrival. Inform them that I have instructed that this unfortunate woman be taken to my room . . . and call a doctor at once."

The speed and authority with which the commands were given momentarily dismayed the usually imperturbable butler, who had been racking his brain trying to reconcile this fine figure of a woman with the vague recollections he had of Lady Katherine. Yet, sensing immediately that this personage was accustomed to obedience and seeming to know exactly what she was about, he made haste to do her bidding.

Katherine did not waste a second in seeing if her instructions were being carried out, but immediately followed Sommers and his burden up the graceful, wide stairway that led to the second floor. She hardly had time to remove her gloves and hat, which she hastily deposited carelessly on a chair, and hurry to the bedside of the stricken woman before the door was flung open and an excited young lady danced into the room.

"Katy, Katy, I'm so glad you're here," the new arrival said breathlessly. She ran toward Katherine, who was waiting for her with outstretched arms. "What's this accident that Reynolds was talking about? You're not hurt, are you?" Gwen's sparkling eyes eagerly scanned Katherine's smiling face.

"No, Gwen dear, no. I'm fine. But this poor woman is still unconscious. Sommers said she stepped right in front of the horses just as we were coming to the door."

The two young ladies, their arms entwined, turned their attention to the still form on the bed as Katherine continued. "I do hope it isn't anything serious for Sommers's sake as well as hers. He's so upset."

"Yes, he would be, poor Sommers . . . poor woman too," said Gwen. "Who is she?"

"I haven't the slightest. Did Reynolds call the doctor?"

"I'm sure he did," Gwen replied. "He said he was going to do just that as he left us. Doctor Harrington only lives a few houses away, and if he's not tied up, he'll be here in a jiff."

Katherine unbuttoned the woman's high-necked bodice and tried to make her as comfortable as possible. The girl moaned and stirred uneasily.

"I do hope the doctor arrives quickly. She seems to be coming 'round," Katherine commented sympathetically. Then, while brushing back her hair, which had been neatly pinned but had now loosened—stray strands dangled across her face—she continued soothingly, "There, there, the doctor will be here any moment. Everything will be all right. Are you in pain?"

Slowly the woman's head turned in the direction of Katherine's blue eyes. "My ankle—just my ankle."

"Well, then, let me look at it, young woman," a brusque voice interrupted. Dr. Harrington had entered the room noiselessly while the two sisters' attentions had been riveted upon the injured woman.

Thankfully, Katherine rose, making room for the doctor, and waited impatiently for him to examine her. He didn't take long.

"No bones broken, but she does have a badly sprained ankle," he addressed the anxious Katherine. "It's too soon to tell about a head injury. I'll wrap up her ankle, but you'll have to make sure she stays in bed, at least 'til I see her in the morning."

Dr. Harrington was a portly gentlemen, his fingers quick, deft, and gentle. His manner expressed professional calm and kindness, and Katherine felt reassured by his diagnosis. Turning to Gwen, she suggested, "Why don't you return to Lady Metcalf and relay the doctor's decision? She must be very concerned. I'll join you as soon as I've seen to everything here. Maybe Betsy could stay with her for a while."

Gwen gave her sister a quick kiss. "You're right, Katy. Oh, it's so, so good to see you. I've missed you . . . I've so much to tell you—"

"Run along now. We'll talk later. Lady Metcalf must be all feathers." Katherine gave her a gentle shove toward the door as she patted her hand affectionately, her gray eyes soft with the genuine love she held for her younger sister.

In the meantime Dr. Harrington had finished bandaging the woman's ankle, and after another quick check stepped back, satisfied that for the moment there was nothing more he could do. During his administrations, the young woman had opened her eyes and watched him, completely bewildered by what was happening.

Katherine accepted a potion from the doctor, listened carefully to his instructions, and then thanked him for his quick response and attention.

"Think nothing of it. Mighty glad to be of service," he replied. With a friendly smile at his patient he continued, "I'm happy that the injury isn't more serious. I'm sure you'll be fine and able to walk as well as ever in a few days. I'll see you again in the morning when I look in on Lady Metcalf."

Having seen the doctor to the door, Katherine returned to the young woman and with a reassuring smile asked her how she felt.

"I'm a little dazed, ma'am, and my ankle does hurt some. But what am I doing here?" Her voice, Katherine noted, was well-modulated and her diction clearly indicated that she was a person of some education, though the style and inexpensiveness of her clothes showed her not to be a woman of means.

"You had an accident in front of Lady Metcalf's home. That's where you are now."

"Lady Metcalf's? Yes, now I remember. I had just gone down the steps and was crossing the street when I noticed the horses. I stepped back, twisted my ankle. I must've fallen."

"I'm afraid my driver made that turn at a spanking clip. I'm so sorry. But did you say you were here at Lady Metcalf's?"

"Yes, ma'am," the young woman answered, nodding. "Yes, I was. I was visiting my cousin Betsy."

"Betsy?" a surprised Katherine interrupted her.

"Yes, ma'am. She's Miss Tarkington's maid."

Katherine smiled, relieved now by the knowledge that the young woman was practically one of the family and not a total stranger. "Yes, that's right. I'm also Miss Tarkington, Katherine Tarkington. And Betsy is more than a maid. She's counted among our friends. Between the three of us, you'll have everything you need to recover from this misfortune in a hurry."

Before the young woman could respond, there was a gentle knock on the door and a neat, elderly woman entered at Katherine's request. A wide, welcoming smile spread across her face as she first sighted Katherine, but it was quickly displaced by an expression of concern as she recognized the figure on the bed.

"Patience, they didn't tell me it was you who had the accident," she wailed as she hurried to the side of her cousin.

Patience smiled weakly in response to her cousin's greeting and hastened to quiet her fears as Katherine explained just what had happened. "In fact, Betsy, I didn't know who she was 'til a minute ago," Katherine said. "But now I'll leave her with you. I must make myself known to Lady Metcalf. Your cousin is to have anything she needs. The doctor said she'll probably take a few days to mend." With an affectionate nod she left the room.

Katherine would have much preferred to refresh

herself after the long journey and the unexpected events of her arrival before joining Lady Metcalf, but dusk had fallen and it would soon be time for dinner. She felt there had already been too long a delay. Besides, the identity of the young woman should be made known to Lady Metcalf at once to arrest any fears she might be harboring, though Katherine was not too concerned on that account, for she was fully aware of Lady Metcalf's generous and thoughtful nature. She had been a bosom friend of her mother's during their childhood. Though Katherine had not seen her often, Lady Metcalf never venturing from the city, her mother's tale of their youthful conquests and happy association, plus her wide reputation for her keen sensitivity, had engendered Katherine's admiration and respect.

The audience passed just as Katherine had expected. Lady Metcalf was all solicitude for the welfare of the injured woman and her newly arrived guest. Her warmth and graciousness enhanced Katherine's already high regard.

Chapter IV

That evening dinner passed with Katherine's regaling her hostess with tales of country life, particularly the activities of the two younger Tarkingtons, which her ladyship heartily enjoyed. Since her fall, Lady Metcalf's active life had been dramatically curtailed, and the presence of the youthful newcomer was a tonic. However, during the course of the dinner Katherine became increasingly aware of the fact that the usually vivacious Gwen, though displaying lively interest in her younger siblings, was not contributing much to the conversation. In fact she was so noticeably subdued that Katherine commented upon her unnatural quietness. Gwen merely laughed, saying that she was exhausted and explaining that it had taken her some time to accustom herself to sleeping late to atone for the many evening festivities, which had lasted into the wee hours of the morning.

Not until the two sisters were in Katherine's room, preparing to retire early, did they find an opportunity for private conversation. Katherine was anxious to listen and Gwen eager to talk.

Katherine sat at her dressing table, brushing her long, luxurious hair, Gwen sprawled on the nearby bed, her violet-blue eyes once again alive and sparkling as she recounted her first ball and her personal triumph. None of Katherine's bitter memories were able to infringe themselves on her delight in her sister's success. There was no jealousy between the two. Each was secure in her own person and sure of the affection, one for the other.

As Gwen continued her recital of her activities, Katherine noticed a bewildered expression settling itself upon her face. Listening carefully, Katherine discovered the cause.

During the first weeks there had been a constant stream of young bucks vying for Gwen's favor. They had flocked around her at the balls, called upon her in the morning, escorted her on afternoon strolls, and cantered with her in the park. For her everything had been as their mother had described.

Then one evening Lord Milford had asked her to dance. Gwen explained that she had made his acquaintance last summer while she was visiting Alice in Bath.

"Maybe you remember, Katy. I think I mentioned him to you then. In fact I'm sure I must have, I was so impressed by him. He seemed such an . . . important person. He was a lot older than the rest and so formal, so correct. Yet after talking to him for a while, I found him to be very pleasant, somewhat like Papa . . . you know what I mean . . . sweet, considerate, and full of warmth."

"No, Gwen, I can't remember your ever mentioning anybody like that—but then you always seemed to have so many beaux to talk about," Katherine answered with a teasing smile. She recalled the conversation she had heard in the inn that very same afternoon. She had had a vague feeling then that the name Milford was familiar. Gwen must have told her about him, but evidently she had attached no importance to him.

"Anyway," Gwen continued, "I had forgotten just how handsome he was. How . . . oh, I don't know how to describe him. He seems so proud, almost arrogant when you look at him, but when he talks to you, he makes you feel so—so warm and good inside. He's a wonderful dancer and, oh, so intelligent. He talks on many different subjects." As Gwen described Lord Milford the vivacious sparkle in her eyes died to a soft, dreamy glow.

Katherine had been watching Gwen closely. She had never before heard her sister speak in such a way about a man. Had Gwen singled out one of her numerous admirers as more desirable than all the others?

"You seem to be developing a tendre for this Lord Milford," Katherine suggested.

"Possibly. Yes, I, suppose I am. Yet he is quite old; he must be twice my age."

Katherine smiled at this offhanded remark. "Near his death bed," she commented.

Gwen giggled. "Don't be silly. He's not that old." She then proceeded to relate what had happened after that fateful night when Lord Milford had first stood up with her. The following morning he called on her and arranged to take her for a drive the next afternoon. He sent her beautiful flowers. In fact he became quite attentive. Once Lord Milford's attentions became obvious, her other beaux slowly dropped away, as if to leave him a clear field. Janet, a friend with whom a fond, confidential relationship had been formed, was enraptured by Gwen's good fortune. Lord Milford was the catch of the season. In fact he had been the catch for many seasons, but beyond a first dance he had never before shown the slightest interest in any of the hopeful young ladies. With civil protestations he had always been able to put off even the most aggressive of mothers.

"Do you mean . . . are you trying to tell me that Lord Milford is . . ." stammered Katherine.

"By all appearance he is going to offer for me," Gwen replied. "At least that is what Janet and Lady Metcalf think. They say he's never dangled after anyone before, and that he's not the type to build up aspirations."

Laying her brush down, Katherine turned toward the bed in order to give her sister her full attention. "And how do you feel about it?" she asked softly.

"Katy, I truly don't know." Gwen hesitated as if taking time to analyze her emotions. "I'm not some scatterbrain looking only for a good time. And though for the most part Lord Milford is terribly serious, he is also kind and considerate. I would be mistress of Milford Hall, with a town house in London or anything else I would possibly want . . . but . . ."

It was obvious to Katherine that others had been enumerating Lord Milford's assets and extolling his virtues. "But what, little sister?" she asked sympathetically.

". . . but . . . I don't know if he really loves me. Or, for that matter, if I love him. I want to be sure, and yet what do I know about love?"

"Love could grow. It could come in time."

"That's what everybody says. Still . . . oh, I don't know," Gwen said and sighed, shrugging her shoulders in frustration.

Katherine responded reassuringly. "Well, don't fret about it, Gwen darling. You don't have to make up your mind yet, and you certainly don't have to marry him if he does offer for you. Once you refuse him, he'll go his way and all your old beaux will come swarming back again."

"But I think I do want to marry him. I'd feel so safe, secure, so protected," replied Gwen, refusing to relinquish the topic that was bedeviling her.

"Haven't any of your other young swains had the gumption to stand up to him?"

At that question Gwen's expression brightened and she laughed. "A couple. But Lord Milford cut them out with such frigid success, they didn't even know what happened. I must say he is a complete hand at the polite setdown." After pausing for a moment in thought, she continued, "Yet, there is one—"

"Oh?" Katherine exclaimed. She listened for a note of interest in Gwen's voice and was disappointed to hear none.

"Lord Leatherton—although he's almost as old as Lord Milford, he seems much younger. I became acquainted with him a few days ago. He's a relative of Milford's, but different in so many ways. Lord Milford is strong-minded and serious, while Leatherton is gay, very witty, and vastly charming—though I've heard he's reputed to be somewhat of a rake. He pays absolutely no attention to Lord Milford. In fact he seems to delight in getting his back up."

The sisters sat in silence for a few minutes, each lost

in her own thoughts. Gwen considered the plight she was in, an enviable one as far as most females of her set were concerned. Katherine worried about her sister, concerned with Gwen's future happiness. She knew how important love in a marriage was to Gwen—no matter how much convention and society ridiculed the idea. Theirs had been a family bathed in affection, their parents obviously devoted to each other. Both Gwen and Katherine had grown up with the idea that their marriages should be nothing less, and Katherine had vowed that she would do all in her power to see to it that Gwen at least would fulfill her dreams.

Katherine broke the silence between them by softly asking, "What are you going to do now?"

Gwen's eyes lit up as a mischievous grin curved her lips. "I am going to run away."

"You're what?" Katherine's surprise and displeasure showed in the abruptness of her tone.

Laughing lightly, Gwen quickly retorted, "Don't look so shocked. Nothing unconventional or improper. Janet has to return home—near Oxford. Her mother is needed. Their nurse has taken it upon herself to get married and leave them, and Janet's mother has to find a suitable replacement. So that Janet won't lose any ground, a big weekend party is being planned. I will just extend my visit until Janet is able to return to London. Heaven knows I can use the rest."

"You minx," scolded Katherine affectionately, "trying to get a rise out of me. But that idea does sound splendid. You'll have some time to think things over. Will Lord Milford be there?"

"Why, of course. A gentleman of his consequence is invited everywhere. The atmosphere will be casual, and he may feel more relaxed. I should get a chance to get to know him better, or I can seek out other company if I've a mind to."

Katherine nodded in appreciation of the sense her younger sister displayed. "When will you be leaving?" she asked.

"Tomorrow morning, early. Lady Metcalf said that we could borrow her carriage; she has no use for it now. Janet wouldn't have room for both of us and our luggage."

Surprised, Katherine stiffened. "You're expecting me to go too? Surely you don't need a chaperon to Janet's family home."

"No, of course I won't need a chaperon," Gwen replied. "I wouldn't have begged you to leave Blue Hills so soon if I had known about this weekend, but now that you're here, I thought you'd—"

"Truthfully, Gwen," Katherine interrupted decisively, "now that I'm here I'd rather stay. I've had enough traveling and I certainly wouldn't relish another jaunt tomorrow, even a short one. I'd be perfectly content to keep poor Lady Metcalf company and just relax . . . maybe take in a concert or go to the theater. They're not closing down, are they, because of the out-of-town competition?"

"No, silly," laughed Gwen. "But I did want you to meet Lord Milford and see what you think of him. You know how I value your opinion."

"There'll be plenty of time for that," Katherine replied with an indifferent wave of her hand. "After all, since I am your guardian, Lord Milford will have to come to me for approval of the marriage. And you can be sure I will know plenty about him before I give my consent."

Though having previously professed fatigue and dire need of a good night's sleep, the two young ladies continued chattering into the late hours.

Chapter V

Accustomed to country living, which meant early rising, Katherine was already awake the following morning when Gwen came tiptoeing into her room to bid her farewell. A few hours sleep and the prospect of a change of scene had been sufficient to bring back the younger sister's exuberance, and as Katherine kissed her good-bye, she felt much easier in her mind. Time and Gwen's own natural resilience would resolve her dilemma.

Unable to go back to sleep, Katherine rang for Sissy to bring her morning chocolate, but it was Betsy who tapped on her door a short time later.

After setting down the tray, Betsy proceeded to draw back the curtains. The sight of the dreary gray mist that shrouded her view brought a moan to Betsy's lips. "More drizzle and fog. The Lord has certainly seen fit to give us more than our share this year."

"It's better than the bitter cold," Katherine murmured pleasantly. Relaxing back on her pillow, she was quite content as she sipped the delicious beverage. "By the way, Betsy, how is your cousin this morning?"

"Oh, much better, Miss Katy. Her ankle's still very painful and swollen, but she says her head is clear and there ain't no other aches. Mighty lucky she was that Sommers was able to stop the horses before they trampled her."

"Really, Betsy," Katherine admonished, "you're being morbid this morning. That would have been horrible, but it didn't happen, so let's not dwell on it. Agatha and Cliff send their love."

Betsy beamed.

"And so does Jamison," added Katherine teasingly.

At that remark Betsy stiffened. Though her face became stern, Katherine could detect the rise of a slightly rosy hue. "You can tell him to mind his vegetables," Betsy replied sharply.

"Now, Betsy, Jamison's a fine gardener and doesn't have to be told what to do," Katherine said.

With an expression of long-suffering patience, the older woman ignored her comment. "Will that be all, Miss Katy? I have plenty to do without standing here listening to your nonsense."

"Touchy . . . sorry, Betsy, I was only funning. But no, there's nothing else right now. Just send Sissy up to me."

Betsy took a few steps toward the door, then hesitated and turned to her mistress. She opened her mouth as if to say something, but shut it without uttering a word.

"Out with it, Betsy," Katherine commanded kindly. Through many years of close association she had learned every one of her companion's moods. "Something's wrong. What is it?"

"You're right, ma'am. It's Patience. She's awfully upset, depressed . . . and she was so happy yesterday. It's unfair how fate works sometimes."

"Upset, depressed, fate? What are you talking about? Doesn't she have everything she needs?"

"Yes, yes. She's right grateful for all you and Lady Metcalf are doing for her. It's just . . . well, she was on her way to a new post when she left here yesterday. She had to go through London so she stopped to tell me all about it. It's all excited and thrilled, she was. Now it looks as if she'll lose the position. She was supposed to arrive there tonight, and there's no way she can do that or even let her new mistress know she can't come or why."

"The poor dear," Katherine responded sympathetically, fully realizing how difficult it was for a young woman to secure a position, particularly one to her liking. "Is there something I can do? Can I get in touch with her employer? Couldn't I send a message explaining the accident and plead that she hold open her post?"

"I suppose you could do that, Miss Katy," Betsy nodded, her face brightening. "A note from you should carry some weight—that is if her new mistress is the kind of lady Patience says she is."

"You go right to her and tell her not to worry. I'll be in for the necessary information as soon as I am dressed. We had best send the message right away."

"Thank you, Miss Katy. I was sure you'd come up with something. I'll tell her right now . . . and I'll send Sissy to you. She'll be ever so grateful."

"Why should Sissy be grateful? I don't imagine she's so anxious to see me."

Betsy started to explain, but seeing the mischievous

twinkle in Katherine's eyes, she tossed her head indignantly and stalked out of the room.

As good as her word, twenty minutes later Katherine entered Betsy's room where Patience had been moved. It was a comfortable little room, naturally not as richly furnished as the guest rooms and now a bit cluttered with the addition of the trundle bed. Still, it was cozier than most servant's rooms, as was befitting the position of the Tarkington sisters' abigail.

Seating herself beside the invalid's bed, Katherine took a more careful look at the young woman, finding her appearance neat and pleasing. She had an ordinary face and Katherine guessed her to be in her late twenties or early thirties, but she had an air of gentleness and composure about her. When she smiled, as she did upon greeting Katherine, she expressed an endearing warmth and friendliness.

"Thank you, milady, for what you are doing for me. This post was an answer to my prayers, and I'd indeed hate to lose it even before I start."

Katherine, aware of the genuine appreciation in her eyes, wanted only to reassure her, but she also realized that many of the fine society ladies would show no consideration for the plight of a mere servant. The slightest inconvenience to them was a personal affront not to be forgiven. "I can't promise to be of any help, Patience, but I am ready to plead your case." Then, smiling, she added, "After all, it was mostly our fault that you find yourself in this predicament. I can embellish on that quite a bit." Turning to her servant, who was standing at the foot of the bed, she said with a conspiratorial smile, "Just don't tell Sommers, Betsy, what a villain I am going to make of him."

"He'll not mind a word you say, Miss Katy, as long as you don't believe it yourself," Betsy replied as she grinned back at her.

Pen and paper in hand, Katherine inquired, "Now what is the name and address?"

"Lady Pamela Wharton, Milford Hall, Bury St. Edmunds, Suffolk . . ."

After writing only the name, Katherine raised an astounded face. "Milford Hall? Is Lady Wharton any relation to Lord Milford?"

"She's his younger sister. And as I understand it, she is now living with him. Her husband died a few years ago. Do you know Lord Milford, ma'am? That would be a—"

"Oh, no, don't get your hopes up too high on that score. I've heard of him but have never met him," Katherine interrupted, tossing a glance at Betsy and noting that the name seemed to have no significance for her. Evidently for once Gwen had not taken the older woman into her confidence.

An idea took shape in Katherine's mind. Who knows better the kind of a person a man really is than the servants in his own house? Abruptly she rose and walked to the window. As if lost in thought, she stared out at the gray dreary mist.

"Just what was your post to be, Patience?" she asked, not turning her head from the window.

"Governess to Lady Wharton's two young sons," she answered, a slight frown creasing her forehead, obviously mystified by Katherine's preoccupation.

Katherine continued to gaze abstractly out of the window, unusual thoughts tumbling around in her head. In this weather she'd not enjoy cavorting about in London. With Gwen gone, she had no responsibilities here. Certainly Lady Metcalf had no pressing need of her. And she was quite capable of being a governess. She could do it! She would pose as Patience and spend a few days right in the lion's den.

Patience's frown deepened as she watched Katherine. Betsy began to stir uneasily.

The more Katherine debated the idea, the better she liked it. After all, since the final decision as to Gwen's marriage rested with her, she would have to know a lot more about the gentleman in question. From the manner in which Gwen spoke of Lord Milford, Katherine was sure that her sister felt deeply about him, but was still uncertain. She, herself, could not be. Yes, she would do it! She must, for Gwen's sake. The prospect was an entertaining one too. Most anything would be better than moping around in London's chilly, dirty dampness. Besides she had never been to Suffolk. It was spring and the countryside would be beautiful, yet quite different than the hills and valleys of Devon.

Suddenly, her mind made up, Katherine turned away from the window, mischief glinting in her eyes. Betsy groaned when she saw that look.

"Patience, I have a plan." A slight smile played about her lips. "And a big favor to ask of you."

Now, even more bewildered, the young woman answered, "Of course, milady, anything I can do—"

"Let me go in your place."

Astonishment widening her eyes, the young woman stared at Katherine. "But, milady! You . . . you're not a—"

"Don't worry about that. I've practically raised three young ones myself."

"But, ma'am, what would I do?"

"You will stay here until you have recovered completely and then . . ." Katherine paused, frowning. "Oh, I see what you mean. Still, I know. I know what we can do," she continued excitedly, her fertile mind speedily amending her plan. "I will arrive at Milford Hall as your substitute until you are on your feet again. Lady Wharton will have someone to be with the children and you will have the post when you are able to assume it."

A puzzled expression clouded Patience's gentle face.

With a satisfied nod of her head, Katherine proceeded to explain the details. "Here is exactly what we will do. It will work," she stated positively. "I, Katherine Tarkington, will write a letter depicting how I caused your accident. Being a responsible person and concerned for your welfare, I have sent my personal abigail to assist Lady Wharton in your stead until you have recovered. Then I will arrive as Betsy the abigail and will explain that since the unfortunate occurence only happened last night there was no way of informing Lady Wharton about it. Since you were so desirous of keeping your position, Miss Tarkington insisted that her personal maid go in your place . . . only I will be she. . . . Simple!"

Speechless, the other two women looked at her in amazement.

"Well?"

"B-b-but, why, Miss Katy?" Betsy finally stuttered.

Smiling secretively at Betsy, Katherine only replied, "I have my reasons, and they're good ones."

"But what of Lord Milford?"

"What do you know about Lord Milford?" Katherine shot a quick sharp retort to her servant.

Still befuddled, Betsy answered hastily, "Nothing, Miss Katy, only that he's called upon Miss Gwen a few times."

Shrugging her shoulders in a gesture of indifference, Katherine commented, "He'll be in Oxford anyway, and if he should return to Milford Hall before I leave, I will certainly be able to stay out of his way." The prospect of Lord Milford's presence had crossed her mind too. It might prove embarrassing to explain at some later date why she had been at Milford Hall posing as a governess to her prospective brother-in-law's nephews. But she dismissed that worry as groundless, remembering that Lord Milford was to be in Oxford for the weekend. Since he was in attendance to Gwen, he surely wouldn't take time off to return to the country during the height of the season. In any case she would only be there for a few days.

Turning her attention to the young woman, Katherine smiled most beguilingly and said, "Say that the plan has your approval, Patience. It would be so advantageous for both of us."

"I don't understand any of this," Patience answered doubtfully, "but if you say so and that's what you want, ma'am, I won't object."

"But I do," Betsy sternly intervened. "Miss Katy, a lady of your position, posing as a governess. It's not to be—"

"Betsy." A warning note in Katherine's tone ended Betsy's objection abruptly.

"I knew it would be no use to say anything, but I

had to try," she submitted, shrugging her shoulders in resignation.

"If I leave right away, I should be able to arrive by nightfall," Katherine continued. "Thank goodness I got up early this morning." All objections cast aside, Katherine was ready for action. "Patience, how did you intend to travel?"

"I have a ticket on the Norwich stage that leaves from Walthamstow. It stops at Bury, where I was to be met."

"Perfect. I'll just use your ticket, then."

Aghast, Betty again objected. "Miss Katherine . . . a common coach. Alone."

Laughing, her eyes dancing with delight, Katherine turned on Betsy. "How many governesses do you know who have their own coaches and travel with maids?"

"None, but—"

"Then it's all settled, Betsy." Again the warning note of authority colored her voice.

"Yes, Miss Katy," Betsy replied, every bit of her disapproval obvious in her tone and manner.

Quickly Katherine's mind sped over the wardrobe she had brought with her. "I'll need one of your bonnets, Betsy, and your cape. My pelisse would be far too grand. I do have a couple of gowns simple enough to be appropriate. Come, Betsy, help me pack."

Chapter VI

Perhaps it was the inclement weather or maybe just the season; nevertheless the coach to Norwich was not crowded, for which Katherine was thankful. Such a trip would have been uncomfortable enough in her own well-sprung barouche. Sitting in the corner next to an oversized member of the clergy, and her knees practically knocking against those of the gaunt, severe-looking woman across from her, Katherine had second thoughts about her venture. These she held only briefly, for what were a few hours of discomfort to matter if she could discover information about Lord Milford that would help her come to a decision about her sister's future?

Gwen had been such a dear child, sweet and unassuming, so eager to brighten her sister's weary hours after the death of their father had foisted so much responsibility on her shoulders. Gwen had never demanded any extra attention or frivolities for herself. Instead she had pitched in with a bright, cheerful nature to do all she could to lighten Katherine's load. Although not one to take charge, she had followed instructions gracefully and without complaint. Now it was time for her reward—a glorious season in London and the right man to take charge of her future. Katherine was determined to make certain that Gwen had them both.

The drizzle changed to heavy rain as they moved farther north, and the damp chilliness permeated the uncomfortable vehicle. As the already leaden gray skies darkened with approaching night, the roads became even more formidable. Their progress had been agonizingly slowed and they were two to three hours behind schedule.

Katherine sighed wearily as she looked out into the gloom, barely able to distinguish the trees through the screen of steadily falling rain. Her first exhilaration, derived from the newfound sense of freedom her impersonation with its loss of position had given her, was fast waning. Her whole body ached from the jouncing she had endured the entire day and was worsening with every revolution of the wheels. The road had become a series of ruts and muddy holes that tested the skill of the driver and the strength of the courageous animals that strained against the elements.

Suddenly the bottom seemed to drop from beneath them; the coach swayed, tipping precariously. As if in a dream, Katherine heard the exasperated shouts of the coachman, and the terrified cries of the horses. The coach settled slowly, the right wheels sinking deep into the mud. There were more shouts and the sharp crack of the whip, but the coach would not budge.

Katherine had been thrown unceremoniously across the obese clergyman, who, in an effort to maintain his own balance, had raised his arms to grasp the side of the coach. As he did so, his heavy hand swung past Katherine's face, knocking her bonnet to the floor to be trampled under his feet as he braced himself. Betsy's bonnet was of little consequence, however, compared to Katherine's safety and dignity.

The unyielding stance of the coach allowed the passengers to right themselves, but before they could adjust to their situation, the door was abruptly opened and the driver stuck in his head, spraying raindrops democratically on the disheveled occupants.

"Wheel's in over its axle. We're stuck, but good. Best you get out and walk. . . ."

Groans of dismay and protest interrupted him.

There was no sympathy in his tired, harassed voice as he continued. "It ain't too far. There's a bit of an inn 'bout a quarter mile. It'll be neat enough. They'll take care of your needs 'til this wagon's back on the road."

Realizing that there was nothing else to do but follow the driver's advice, the disgruntled passengers descended. Katherine was thankful that she had worn Betsy's sensible cape, which would provide sufficient protection against the rain. But what about her hair? Her bonnet would be in no condition to wear, even if she could retrieve it.

There was nothing she could do about that either, so resolving to make the best of the situation, Katherine gripped her reticule tightly and fell in beside the driver as he started off down the road. They had not gone far when a change of mood slowly developed within Katherine. She found that the rain, which had so depressed her earlier, was now a soft spring rain that tapped gently against her. The air was fresh and bracing. Often she had purposely donned an old cloak and boots to walk through the pastures at Blue Hills in just such weather, relishing the clean, washed scent of the air and the sensuous delight of the rain on her face. These same exhilarating emotions lifted her spirits now. It was a relief as well to stretch her muscles after being cramped all day in the corner of the jouncing coach.

With her head high and a half smile on her face, Katherine thoroughly enjoyed herself as she sloshed along beside the driver through the darkness, the rain, and the mud underfoot. There was no need to pick her way, for after two strides her slippers had been soaked through and the hem of her gown totally drenched. Yet it seemed to Katherine that all too soon soft, fuzzy lights were beckoning to them through the rain. Almost with disappointment, she permitted the driver to assist her through the gate and up the short path leading to the inn.

"At least you seem to be enjoying this, miss." He spoke gruffly, but there was a twinkle of admiration in his eye.

"I like the rain," Katherine answered with a flashing smile.

"Well, it does have a way of upsetting plans and schedules," he commented ruefully as he pushed open the door to the inn and stepped aside to allow her to enter first.

Though Katherine had not minded the cold, the warmth of the public room greeted her pleasantly. The odors of baked bread and sweet wines that suddenly assailed her nostrils reminded her that she had not eaten. The fresh air had given her an oversized appetite. The room was bright, noisy, and cheerful. The coachman had been right—it appeared to have everything to care for their needs.

A plump, elderly woman scurried toward them with a cheery, welcoming smile on her round face. "Come on in out of the weather," she invited heartily.

Katherine froze as the eyes of the older woman met hers and a look of astonishment swept across her face. Katherine frowned, pursed her lips, and shook her head from side to side ever so slightly. "Thank you for your welcome, ma'am," she said. Then, in lowered tones for the old woman's ears alone, she added crisply, "You don't know me."

"Oh, milady, but—"

"Don't 'milady' me," Katherine interrupted softly but with authority. "I'll explain later."

The older woman started to dip in a curtsy but was restrained by Katherine's quick shake of her head and a gentle hand on her arm.

The other passengers had entered, and the driver explained their difficulties to the innkeeper, a small neat man who had taken his place next to the plump woman who had greeted them.

"My wife and I will do all we can to accommodate you," he said as he smiled sympathetically at the bedraggled newcomers. "We're a little short of room, but we don't lack for good food and drink. As you can see, you're not the only ones delayed by this infernal weather."

While they were talking, Katherine had noticed that the common room was already quite full—the benches by the hearth occupied by a large family. A tired-looking woman cradled an infant in her lap while a couple of young ones fidgeted at her feet. A harassed man, probably her husband, was overseeing the activities of two bigger boys, who were rebelling against the confinement of a bench by the fire.

Katherine would have liked to change places with them. Though Betsy's cloak had kept most of her warm and dry, her feet in her wet slippers were fast becoming chilled as she stood on the cold stone floor, and her hair, thoroughly soaked, sent continuous rivulets down her face.

The innkeeper's wife, aware of Katherine's discomfort, turned to her husband. "Surely milord would not object to sharing his fire with this poor drowned young one."

The little man looked at her and shrugged. "He left orders he was not to be disturbed," he replied. But after taking stock of Katherine's sodden condition and mindful of further urgings from his wife, he continued, "But milord's a fair man and 'tis sure I am that he'd not be wanting you to catch your death on his account."

After quickly seating the other two passengers, the innkeeper indicated to Katherine to follow him as he wended his way through the crowded room. Instantly his wife was at Katherine's side.

"What's this all about, Miss Katy?" she whispered sternly.

With a mischievous sparkle in her eyes, Katherine held a finger to her lips. "Not now, Charity. There's no time to explain. Just don't give me away. Only remember, I'm a governess taking on a new position near here."

"'A governess? Oh, my . . . Miss Katy." Wonder and dismay colored the woman's voice.

A feeling of warmth and affection flowed through Katherine as she saw the worry in the older woman's face. How she wanted to reach over and kiss those round red cheeks as she had done so often as a tiny girl, begging for cookies in the kitchen.

"Really, Charity, everything is all right." Katherine reassuringly patted the plump arm.

In the meantime the innkeeper had knocked gently on a door at the end of the room and opened it in response to a command from within.

"Pardon, milord, but the stage has had an accident," the innkeeper explained to the room's occupant. "The passengers have had to walk for a ways here and we are quite full up. Would you be willing to allow this young miss to dry herself by your fire here? She's near drowned, that she is, sir."

Coming up behind the innkeeper, Katherine examined the man he had addressed. He was standing by the hearth with his back toward them, seemingly staring into the fire, one raised arm resting on the mantel. He was taller than average and his broad shoulders were encased in a fine cloth coat that was stretched tight across his back and accented his strength. Buckskins and high boots, whose shine brightly reflected the ruddy glow of the fire, completed his attire, which was somewhat somber but elegant and in excellent taste. His own thick black hair was tied neatly at the nape of his neck. A very impressive figure of a man, Katherine judged—from the back anyway.

Without turning, he merely grumbled indifferently, "I suppose so. If you feel it's necessary." His deep voice was cold and plainly showed his annoyance.

Immediately Katherine took offense. Such an arrogant, thoughtless boar! He was not the least concerned about the misfortunes of others. She would certainly not disturb him. She'd give him her opinion of him and leave him to his own insufferable company. Just as she was about to commence her setdown, she remembered the crowded conditions of the common room and her own humble position. She composed herself. There were other ways to take him down a notch. A tiny smile played at the corner of her lips as she decided upon other tactics. With an elaborate, low curtsy and in the nasal tones copying the accent of the rustics, she said, "Oh, la, milord, I do thank you. 'Tis true I'm just about done in. Me bonnet's lost and me hair's nothing but a soaked rat's nest."

Charity gasped in amazement.

The gentleman turned at the sound of her voice and looked down at the brown-cloaked figure huddled in bent subservience.

"Go over to the fire. You won't get any drier over there," he commanded curtly.

"Oh, thank you, milord," she said as she raised her face to his. There was no humbleness there, only a dazzling smile.

He caught his breath as he gazed at that lovely face. The smooth white skin glowed from the rain, the full red lips spread in a tantalizing smile glistened in the firelight, the eyes sparkled with laughter.

"Milord," an agitated Charity intervened. "This is—

she hesitated, looking at Katherine—"is Miss Hope Bottomsly. She's to take a post near here."

Rising from her curtsy, Katherine shot a glance at Charity. Why that name? She was sure she had caught a glint of sly satisfaction in Charity's eyes. She had given Katherine her own maiden name, one which the Tarkington youngsters had heartlessly made fun of many a time. Katherine laughed to herself. *She's getting back at me now,* she thought, *saddling me with Miss Bottoms-up or Mistress Roundbottom.*

"Your servant." The gentleman awarded the introduction with civility and chilly aloofness, then turned to the innkeeper. "I hope my supper will not be delayed."

"No, sir. Just a few minutes now, milord."

"Supper! La-de-da, I'm right starved. Me stomach's rumbling like a bear crossing a bridge," Katherine exclaimed, rubbing her stomach energetically. Her eyes widened with beseechment, she pleaded, "Might you spare me a bit?"

Confusion showed plainly on the innkeeper's face. This was unheard of—a mere nobody imposing her company on a gentleman.

"Bring the young woman something to eat, James." With that command the gentleman turned his back and walked away, apparently finished with the present company.

Katherine's indignation continued to mount. She supposed she should have been grateful, but his tone, his manner—what condescension, how boorish. Well, before this evening was out, she would show him just how uncouth one could be. Again her face lit up with excited pleasure. "La, you're too kind. I ain't going to be no bother to you, I promise." But a bother she did intend to be!

After the innkeeper and his wife left the room, Katherine removed her wet cape and hung it over the back of a chair, carefully spreading its folds so it would dry quickly. "I'll just toast meself by the fire a bit," she continued. She moved gracefully over to the hearth and sat down on an ottoman, stretching out her feet and hands to the dancing flames.

"La, what a scare we had. I'll tell you," she exclaimed. "The coach just swayed, then sunk. Thought we'd never hit bottom. I was throwed across this big preacher. . . ." As she jabbered on, embellishing every weary detail, she did not take her eyes from the fire, but she could feel him watching her—in exasperation, she hoped.

In the middle of her description of her descent from the coach, she abruptly changed subjects. "Goodness gracious. I've brought half the mud from the road here into this fine room." Bending forward, she removed her ruined slippers. "Look at this, will you?" she commanded in a shrill nasal voice as she held up a muddy shoe for his inspection. "My mistress must've bled a few quid for this. It's no good to no one now." She tossed the offending object on the floor near the fire.

The gentleman had not uttered one word. He had not had the opportunity, even if he had desired to do so, as Katherine rambled on, scarcely pausing for breath.

Though the warmth of the fire had made short work of the chill in Katherine's hands and feet, it had little effect on her thick hair, which was pulled primly into a bun at the nape of her neck. With a complete disregard of her last comment, she raised her hand to her hair and complained in disgust, "It's like a sponge. It'll never dry tied up in a knot like this." With deft movements she removed the pins, letting the long heavy tresses fall over her shoulders.

"Ohhh," she shrieked. "It's cold 'n' wet." She moved closer to the fire and rumpled her hair briskly. "That's better . . . this feels so good, so warm." Drawing a brush from her reticule, Katherine cocked her head to one side and with long sensuous movements began to stroke the glistening dark locks.

Katherine's only intention had been to vex his lordship—to pay him in kind for what she considered his arrogant insensibilities to the plight of others. She never considered that her actions might have any other effect, for she had no idea of what an extremely entrancing picture she made, her natural loveliness enhanced by the soft glow of the firelight.

Finally she turned and flashed a gay, uninhibited smile at him. "It was so good of you, milord, to let the likes of me share your fire."

"It's nothing . . . nothing," he muttered, his eyes captured as if bewitched by the scene before him.

His lordship began to pace restlessly. Katherine wondered what was in his mind. He seemed agitated, angered. Well, good, that's what she had intended.

Katherine's continued incessant chatter—any trivial bit of nonsense that came to mind—was interrupted by a sharp knock on the door, and a young serving maid entered carrying a well-loaded tray. As she set the covers on the table, Katherine scrambled from her seat on the ottoman and unceremoniously slipped into a chair, quickly pulling it up to the table, heedless of the gentleman's attempt to assist her.

"Lordy, this smells yummy," she sang out in praise, "but I would just as well welcome last week's Kiplings, that hungry I be."

With an indifferent shrug, the gentleman languidly sat down at the table. First a look of amazement and then amusement spread over his face as he watched Katherine unfashionably heap her plate high.

Katherine stuffed her mouth ravenously but still managed to utter words of praise for every bite of food. And it was delicious too; she had known it would be. Hadn't Charity been cook at Blue Hills for most of the first seventeen years of Katherine's life? She remembered the many times she had sneaked into the kitchen to beg for handouts between meals. She remembered too the happy, but tearful good-bye when, late in the middle years of Charity's life, the sweetheart of her youth had finally inherited his father's inn and had enough money to claim Charity as his bride.

Though it may have appeared that Katherine gave her entire concentration to the food before her, in truth she kept a sly watch on the gentleman and inwardly laughed in triumph at the slight frowns of annoyance that frequently creased his brow.

Nevertheless she had to admit that he covered his irritation well as he ate quietly, only agreeing with her loquacious praise in monosyllabic replies. Upon noting that Katherine had finished her wine, he even refilled her glass.

"Ta, milord. Didn't I say you was the kindest person ever?" She swallowed a gulp of the fragrant beverage.

Licking her lips in delight, she exclaimed, "That's delicious . . . almost as good as we have back at Blue Hills."

At the mention of Blue Hills, the gentleman arched his eyebrows in question.

Katherine caught his expression of interest and needed no prompting to expound. "Have you heard of Blue Hills? It's my mistress's place in Devon. La, 'tis beautiful there. We have such fine lands, acres and acres. . . ." She continued to extol the wonders of her home. In describing the scenes she loved so much, her voice became softer and her speech more gentle.

"You liked your position there?" he asked pleasantly, his manner responding to the change in Katherine.

"La, yes. 'Tis like me very own home. The two young ones give me a run for me life, but they're just normal, healthy yearlings. . . ." Katherine rambled on to tales of her own younger days, depicting her own carefree, mischievous behavior as that of her present charges. She even confessed the ridiculous twists they had given her name, the merciless teasing she had undergone. Thinking back over those days, Katherine realized what a time poor Betsy and Charity must have had.

She was unaware of it but the atmosphere between them had altered. As if caught by her enthusiastic, happy reminiscences, his lordship joined the conversation, paralleling her experiences with his own and the antics of his two young nephews he had witnessed. His eyes softened in shared amusement as he matched her, scandalous behavior for scandalous behavior.

When the maid brought in their coffee, she had

some difficulty in hiding her surprise at the cordiality between the two as she glanced, unnoticed, from one to the other.

As Katherine prepared to serve the coffee, she suddenly remembered the role she had assumed and, managing to instill a bit of awkwardness into her movements, spilled a bit of the brew into the saucers. His lordship gave her actions no heed, smiling appreciatively as he accepted his cup.

Maybe she had been too hasty in her judgment of this man, Katherine thought as she surveyed him over the brim of her cup. He certainly was handsome, and now, there was none of the earlier arrogance that had antagonized her originally. He was relaxed and seemed to be thoroughly enjoying himself. She realized, with a start, that she too felt at ease and—for some unknown reason—extremely happy. This wasn't what she had intended. But then, she reflected, he was acting like any heartless animal. Once well fed, he was content.

"Oh," Katherine snorted distastefully, "this cream's mighty thin . . . tastes little better'n water." A little charm and a few smiles weren't going to get him off the hook.

"You think so? It seems fine to me," his lordship responded.

"'Spose this is as rich as one can expect from the likes of those 'round here."

A wry smile twisted the gentleman's lips. "So you do better in Devon?"

"Lordy, yes! Devon cream's the best! The whole world knows that. Our farming methods are right smack up to the times."

"Meaning?"

"Well, I've heard that East Anglia farmers are no better than backward peasants. Even though Lord Townshend hailed from Norfolk, the yokels around here are all too stubborn to see the value of his methods, even though he planted his first turnip over fifty years ago. Bet you've never even heard of Blakewell."

"Blakewell? Who's he?"

With that question they again found themselves involved in discussion—not about childish pranks now, but the serious business of profitable farming. The conversation became animated as they hit upon point after point in which they were not in agreement. Katherine, sure in her knowledge, had no qualms in belittling his methods and ideas. Though new to farming and well aware that he had much to learn, his lordship was unused to this kind of high-handedness, particularly from a mere female. Suddenly he rose to his feet, all his former hauteur returned.

"How is it that you, a mere servant, consider yourself to be an authority on such matters?" His tone was cool and sarcastic.

Katherine gasped. In her zeal had she overplayed her hand, given herself away? Yet how dare he use that tone with her. He had called her a mere servant! Her resentment of his male superiority overcame her prudence, and she replied frigidly, "My mistress took a great interest in the estate. When her poor father was put underground, she took over its management and I—helped her." Matching his arrogance, Katherine rose and, with exaggerated dignity, marched over to the fireplace.

His lordship watched her retreating figure and impulsively followed her as if to continue their argument. As he stepped behind her Katherine, not realizing that he was there, turned abruptly and found herself bumping against him. Instinctively he put out his hand to steady her. Her head was tilted back, her mouth slightly open as she was about to make some scathing remark, but the words died on her lips as their eyes met, locked.

Suddenly his arms were around her, pressing her to him. His mouth covered hers. There was no resistance. At first Katherine had been too startled by his nearness to oppose him. Then she didn't want to, for within her she felt a pounding, a racing, a roaring she had never before experienced. It was exciting, exhilarating, but also frightening when she realized that she was responding to his kiss—her first real kiss, by a gentleman who thought she was a servant. How could she have become involved in a situation so insane! She jerked herself free.

"How dare you!" she raged at him. There was both anger and fright in her eyes.

Abruptly his lordship dropped his arms, stepped back, and looked at her with an expression of surprise and puzzlement.

Confused and angered, Katherine rushed toward the door, seeking escape. As she reached for the knob she heard his voice.

"Miss Bottomsly," he spoke softly. "Maybe you had better think twice before making an entrance into a very crowded public room—looking as you do. Sans shoes, hair down, and in a rather agitated state of mind."

Slowly she lowered her hand as the picture of herself he had drawn formed in her mind. He was right. If Lady Metcalf or anyone of her circle could see her now. . . . What had she done? Compromised . . . no, no, of course not. She had done nothing, nothing at all, she told herself as she breathed deeply, calming herself and regaining her composure.

Her head held high, but without looking at him, she retraced her steps to the fireplace, sat down on the ottoman, and proceeded with deliberation to put on her slippers, which were stiff and still a trifle damp. This simple act helped her to recover from her first feelings of shock at her own emotions and reactions. Her sense of humor again managed to assume control as she imagined all sorts of hilarious revelations that could be circulated by her acquaintances if they only knew. . . .

"I hope you don't expect me to apologize. I'm not the least bit sorry." His lordship's gentle but slightly mocking voice interrupted her reflections.

Of course not, she thought. Kissing a servant was of no consequence to him.

"I didn't expect you to. I imagine 'tis quite a pastime with you, milord," she replied indignantly as she coiled her hair tightly and replaced the pins.

"As a matter of fact it hasn't been. If I had known it would be so delightful, I might have started sooner."

"'Tis a rather simple feat for milord to force—"

"I didn't force. You asked for that." But before they could continue, a knock interrupted them.

Opening the door, the innkeeper nodded first to the gentleman, and then directed his voice to Katherine. "There's more unfortunate news, Miss B.—Bottomsly."

Katherine smiled as he stumbled over the name and wondered if Charity had informed him of her real identity, but she merely answered with a quizzical, "Yes?"

"The stage driver has just returned and reports that the wheel's broken. There'll be no traveling tonight."

"Nooo, I was supposed to take up my new post tonight," Katherine moaned, fearful that her adventure might cost poor Patience her position after all.

With a sympathetic shrug, the innkeeper continued, "And I'm sorry, but there's not an extra room in the place either. My missus says you might share the young maid's room . . . if you've a mind to. There's nothing else."

Before Katherine could reply, his lordship spoke. "That won't be necessary, James. She may have my room. I'll stretch out before the fire in here. Tell my man to bring down my things immediately."

Katherine bristled at the autocratic tone he had again assumed. Besides, she did not want to become more involved with him or to be beholden to him. Quickly she intervened her protests, but the innkeeper only nodded to the gentleman and paid her no heed.

"As you say, sir," he agreed. "I'm sure we can make everything quite comfortable for you in here, Lord Milford."

"Lord Milford," Katherine repeated, her voice husky with shock. Her eyes filled with horrified surprise, she stared at him while her thoughts tumbled every which way in her mind. The color drained from her face and she felt herself trembling. Now what had she done? Was this the man who was to offer for her sister? Had she already jeopardized her position as his future sister-in-law?

His lordship took hold of her arm to steady her. "Miss Bottomsly, what's wrong?"

Katherine struggled for composure while her mind raced. What should she tell him? Should she end this escapade right now? How could she explain to Lord Milford and still maintain her dignity? No! She hadn't accomplished her purpose. She was not a quitter.

"I'm sorry," she apologized, still a little shaky. "I'll be all right. I just felt a sudden chill."

"I hope you're not going to suffer any ill effects from your stroll in the rain."

"No, I'm sure I won't. I'll be all right in the morning. All I need is a bit of a rest." Then pausing to gather her courage, she asked as matter-of-factly as she could, "Did the innkeeper call you Lord Milford?"

"Yes, I am Lord Milford."

"Lady Wharton's brother?"

"The same."

Katherine could not control an escaping moan.

"Was there a particular reason why you asked?" Lord Milford queried as he watched her speculatively.

"Well—my destination is Milford Hall . . . I—"

"You're the new governess my sister is expecting," he finished for her. There was amusement in his tone.

"Ahhh, yes . . . and no." As Katherine stammered her answer, her mind worked at a feverish pace. She had to continue just as planned. It was too late to change anything now. She would worry about explanations at a later day if any were necessary.

"Yes. No. Which is it?" he asked. "Truthfully you're

not exactly the type I would expect to be governess to two young boys."

Though Katherine was aware of the impression she had tried to give him and how well she had succeeded, she bristled at the raillery in his voice. "I'm quite qualified, milord," she snapped back at him, "but that's beside the point. No, I am not the governess Lady Wharton expected. I'm to take her place until she's fit to come herself."

"A substitute governess! Isn't that a—unusual for one with all your talents?"

From his tone Katherine knew he was mocking her. How she wanted to lash back at him and his superiority! What did he know about governesses? But this was not the time to be concerned about her own feelings.

"Patience, the young woman Lady Wharton was expecting," Katherine replied coolly, now fully in command of herself, "is my cousin and was visiting me when she had an accident. In fact me mistress felt she caused it and sent me to take her place until poor Patience recovers. It's all here right in this letter . . . " She reached into her reticule to find the letter she, as Miss Katherine Tarkington, had written.

Just as she was about to draw out the missive, she remembered that she had signed her full name as befitting her position in writing a letter of reference. What connection would Lord Milford draw from that signature? Katherine wasn't ready to chance any more complications and, after a couple more seconds of futile search, continued in perplexed tones, "Oh, where is it? Did I put it in my valise?"

"Never mind. It's not me you'll have to satisfy but Lady Wharton. But when will the right person be available?"

Relieved in the knowledge that Lord Milford had, at least on the surface, accepted her story, she now faced him with more confidence. "I'm not sure, milord. She's got a sore ankle and couldn't walk. Me thinks that was the worst of her pains."

The innkeeper had stepped back courteously during the exchange but listened avidly. His face bore an expression of extreme interest, but he reacted quickly to Lord Milford's mild command.

"Didn't I ask you to tell Parker to bring my things? And also have Miss Bottomsly's luggage taken to my— her room. She won't be leaving with the stage tomorrow." He turned again to Katherine and added, "I'll probably be leaving early in the morning. You can accompany me."

"Yes, milord. Thank you, milord," Katherine bent her head and dipped in a slight curtsy. She would have to remember that she was a servant and act accordingly. Her sense of humor was returning now that all the hurdles seemed to have been successfully overcome. She glanced shyly at his lordship, a merry twinkle in her eye.

Lord Milford had been watching her intently, and when he caught the sparkle in her eye, he responded with a roguish glance of his own. "You're feeling better now?"

Before Katherine could answer, Parker arrived, ladened with cases and outer apparel.

"Your things, milord." If he was surprised at the turn of events, there was no evidence in his face or tone as he set the cases on a small table and carefully hung the great coat with its layers of capes.

"Parker, do you think the bridge will be usable by eight in the morning?"

"If eight's when you said it was to be fixed, then it will be fixed by eight."

Lord Milford nodded and turned to Katherine. "You can be ready by eight?"

"Yes, of course."

"We'll breakfast at seven, then. Parker, show Miss Bottomsly to her room."

Katherine, eager to have done with his lordship's company before any new complications might arise, followed Parker through the coffee room to a small hall and up a narrow flight of stairs. The room to which Parker guided her was a splendid one for such a small inn. Evidently a number of the gentry must have made a practice of stopping here. It was large, sparkling clean, and simply but tastefully furnished.

Immediately upon following Parker into the room, the maid who had served them earlier came in behind them.

"Lord Milford says I was to help you if you need anything, miss."

Surprised, Katherine gave her a searching look. "No, I can't think of anything. Thank you anyway."

"Yes'm." The little maid gave a quick curtsy from habit and scurried away, as if she feared Katherine might change her mind and find something for her to do.

Turning to Parker, who had been leaning indolently against the doorway, Katherine looked at him questioningly. So far the small wiry man had not said a word. "Is your master always so concerned about the welfare of his help?"

Katherine noticed his eyes light up and a bit of a smile tug at the corner of his lips. "Milord's a fair man, miss. But he don't hardly take this kind of trouble with just servants."

Katherine didn't miss his meaning, as the light in his eye grew to a knowing gleam. Resentment of his obvious thoughts rose within her, but what could she say? Evil minds would jump to their own conclusions. Or did he, knowing his master, suspect that the changing of luggage was just a front? Did he suspect his lordship of other intentions?

"Thank you, Parker. Would you please leave now. I've had a very trying day." Katherine dismissed him icily.

"Why to be sure, miss." She was certain that his smile had become a leer.

The instant the door closed, Katherine hurried to lock it but found no key. Was she herself jumping to conclusions? Just what kind of a man was Lord Milford? He was a gentleman—or was he? Hadn't he already taken the liberty of kissing her once tonight? Did he have the key to the room? Was there a key? These questions plagued her. Should she go to Charity and ask for the key? No, any more fuss might lead to some embarrassing questions.

Katherine surveyed the room and espied what she needed. With cold determination she proceeded to barricade the door with a heavy chair piled with her two cases. Anyone could still force his way into the room but would make plenty of noise in doing so. Her screams would do the rest.

Satisfied with her precautions, Katherine completed her preparations for retiring and was soon curled under the fluffy down quilt. For a short while her mind retraced the events of the day but constantly focused and refocused on the picture of Lord Milford's face as he bent to kiss her. An unknown emotion stirred her—one she couldn't quiet.

Gwen had said he was polite and considerate, but too serious. Katherine had found him, at first, arrogant and insensitive, but then later, amusing and intelligent. Finally, she had to admit, she felt him to be disturbing. Was this the same man who was about to offer for her sister? Was she to decide if he would make a suitable husband for Gwen? A chill enveloped her when she posed the question.

Chapter VII

Exercising self-discipline, Katherine finally managed to push aside her thoughts and was soon asleep, not to be disturbed until the little serving maid knocked smartly on her door the next morning.

"Six thirty, miss," she called out brightly.

Katherine mumbled a sleepy thanks.

"Can I do anything for you?"

Still half asleep, Katherine replied, "No, thank you. I'm sure you have plenty else to do."

"That I have."

Katherine could hear the maid's quick, retreating steps as she rose to a sitting position, stretched, and yawned. Catching sight of the stacked chair against the door, the events of the previous evening returned to her. Nothing had happened during the night. No one had tried to enter the room. So she had been guilty of overreacting—of jumping to conclusions. She smiled and sank back down on her pillow in thought. She felt the blood rising to her face when she became aware of both the relief and disappointment she experienced. What was happening to her? She had never harbored such outlandish thoughts before.

The room was chilly from the early morning air.

Katherine dressed quickly, frowning at the muddy stains around the hem of her gown. She had carefully brushed and hung the gown the night before, but it was not in very good condition. Still, it would look more presentable than one taken from her valise. Her slippers were stiff and thoroughly unwearable. Thank goodness she had another pair handy. Having preferred to tend to her own needs most of her young, independent life, Katherine was quite able to ready herself in short time for the final lap of the journey to Milford Hall.

When she again entered the private parlor, Charity was already there attending Lord Milford. Places had been set for two, and his lordship had already begun to eat. Charity greeted her with such a worried look in her eye that Katherine felt guilty at not being able to give her old friend a reassuring explanation. Lord Milford's presence prohibited that. Instead she extended her a warm smile and, in the nasal tones of the character she had adopted, expressed her delight with her room and the delicious aroma of the food before her.

"I hope everything will be all right, miss," Charity responded, not at all appeased by Katherine's compliments.

"Everything will be fine. There's no need for you to concern yourself about anything . . . about anything at all." Katherine gave her an affectionate pat on the arm.

His lordship had risen upon Katherine's entrance, and after having civilly greeted her, he returned his full attention to his breakfast. The unusual warmth of their exchanged glances went unnoticed.

Still undecided as to exactly how she was going to

conduct her masquerade, Katherine ate quickly and silently. The less said to Lord Milford, the less she would have to worry about later. In any case, the gentleman seemed to be in haste to complete the meal and be on his way.

Less than a half hour later Katherine was seated beside Lord Milford in his smartly styled curricle. She viewed with admiration the two beautiful matched grays that pawed the ground, impatient to be on their way. His lordship had outfitted himself up to the mark as far as his horseflesh was concerned, and her appreciation of his ability as a whip mounted as he expertly handled the reins, allowing the grays to dash forward at their own speed. The narrow, winding road was still muddy from the recent rains, so Milford's attention was necessarily given over to the task of driving.

Nevertheless they proceeded at a smart clip, Katherine absorbed in the tranquil beauty of the gently sloping meadows and small patches of newly leaved trees. The freshness of the brisk morning air enlivened her. After traveling a mile or so, she became aware that, although there had been a few sheep and cattle quietly foraging in the pastures, there had been no dwellings or any sign of human habitation.

She finally broke the silence. "'Tis a lonesome road," she said.

"It is not exactly a road," Lord Milford responded. "More a driveway. It leads only to Milford Hall—a back entrance. Coming from London, it eliminates the need of going on to Bury and then backtracking."

"Then, this is all your property?"

"Part of the estate, yes."

They continued on in silence and Katherine took the opportunity to study the man beside her. Besides being very wealthy—at least a great landowner—he certainly was handsome, but as Gwen had mentioned, past his first youth. He possessed the bearing of maturity and authority. What fine eyes he had, she thought as she noted their concentration on the road ahead. A square, firm chin; a high, broad forehead; heavy dark brows; a straight, narrow nose—a most pleasing masculine countenance. Quickly Katherine looked away to the swiftly passing scene, suddenly discomforted to find that she was breathing fast and that her blood was racing. Yes, he was rich, handsome, and, as far as Katherine was concerned, exceptionally disturbing.

Soon they approached a swollen stream and Lord Milford slackened the pace a bit until he spied a young lad standing by a bridge hailing him on. Tossing him a friendly salute, his lordship gave the grays their head again and they thundered over the wooden planks. Katherine remembered Parker's comment. "If his lordship said the bridge was to be fixed by eight, so it would be." Evidently Lord Milford's commands were executed with alacrity.

Aside from the disturbing emotions her scrutiny of Lord Milford had raised, Katherine enjoyed the ride tremendously. She herself was quite capable of driving such a team, and it was with the knowledge of experience that she admired the skill with which he handled this spirited twosome. She relished the speed. The air was cool, but the sun was bright and warm. As the rain the night before had pleasured her, the wind that now flayed her face and tugged at her hair excited her.

As the horses had at first beat their fast tattoo on the muddy ground, they were now pounding on a more solid gravel terrain.

"Hang on," his lordship warned as he flourished his whip high above the heads of the grays. Knowing well the territory and with the liveliness inbred in them, the horses responded, willingly leaping forward with a jolt that almost upset Katherine. The grays took the next sharp turn without the slightest slackening of their speed, and in a few breathtaking moments Lord Milford pulled on the reins and called them to a halt.

Katherine had loved every second of the spirited dash. Exhilarated, she turned glowing eyes to his. "Oh, that was capital. You are a hand, milord!"

"Why thank you, Miss Bottomsly." He returned her smile, his eyes again taking in the fresh loveliness of her face, the sparkling zest in her eyes. There was admiration in his glance as he remarked, "You seemed to have enjoyed the ride. You weren't frightened?"

"Oh, no, milord," Katherine answered emphatically and quickly added breathlessly in way of explanation, "My mistress is as fine a whip as most gentlemen, sir, and I accompany her often."

He eyed her speculatively. "Someday I would like to meet this paragon of a mistress."

Again on the alert to be mindful of her tongue, Katherine answered in a subdued tone, "That's hardly likely, sir. She seldom leaves the country."

As the grays jolted to a stop, two grooms had immediately rushed to their heads. His lordship jumped to the ground and exchanged friendly greetings with them, then aided Katherine's descent. In her excitement she had not taken time to note her surroundings, but she did so now. The road they had traveled ended in front of the stables, and his lordship proceeded to lead her through a cluster of shrubs and trees. They made a sharp turn and with a few steps emerged from the leaf-filtered light of the woods into brilliant sunshine. Katherine had her first sight of the manor house that was Milford Hall. She gasped at its beauty. The Georgian-styled red brick building was larger, yet more compact, than Blue Hills, but her first impression, in spite of its size, was of a homey snugness. Whereas Blue Hills had spacious lawns with the blue haze-covered hills as a background, Milford Hall nestled among terraced gardens and shrubs and trees of every size and shape. Each was magnificent in its own way.

Lord Milford wasted no time in admiring the scene before him but immediately propelled her toward the manor. Climbing the steps of a small side entrance, he stopped abruptly, and after looking her over, quite brazenly commented, "It might be best if you make yourself more presentable before Lady Wharton interviews you—and be sure you have your mistress's letter with you. Without it, I doubt if you will stay very long."

Instinctively Katherine stiffened at his words and autocratic tone, but as her hand flew quickly to her hair she understood his meaning. The winds had loosened it, and long wisps were flying every which way.

Lord Milford took one of the soft dark locks and gently rolled the fine strands between his fingers. "For myself, I rather like it this way or, better still, the way you wore it last night," he murmured softly.

Katherine froze. That same pounding, that same

racing that she had experienced when he had kissed her again assailed her. Raising her eyes to his, she felt herself helplessly swaying toward him. He released the lock of hair and cupped her shoulders with his hands, gently pulling her to him. His smoldering gaze locked with hers, and as he slowly bent his head toward her he again saw that startled look of wonder and fear in her eyes. Katherine waited as if in a trance. She had delighted in a ride that might easily have killed her but was petrified by a mere embrace. Abruptly he dropped his hands and stepped away. Opening the door, he stepped aside and indicated that she should enter.

Katherine's mind, as if released from a spell, was in a whirl. She had always prided herself on her complete self control. Never before had she had the slightest difficulty in thwarting the amorous advances of aspiring males, young or old. But never before had she been in the presence of one whose very nearness seemed to leave her mind bereft of coherent thought. Never before had she desperately wanted to be kissed, but she was terrified by the strange racing of her heart, the pounding in her head, her feeling of absolute helplessness.

With her eyes lowered, Katherine stepped into the house. Lord Milford followed her into a small vestibule that was the juncture of three hallways. Striding down the corridor to his left, he pushed open one of the doors. "I don't know where your room will be, but for now you can use this one."

"Thank you, milord." Her eyes still downcast, she bobbed him a slight curtsy.

"I'll inform Lady Wharton of your arrival and explain the substitution."

"Thank you again, milord. You're too kind. I took care last night to find me mistress's letter. 'Tis handy now. I won't be needing but a few minutes . . . but where am I to go?" With a problem to attack, Katherine's normal composure quickly returned.

"I'll send a maid to direct you. Shall we say fifteen minutes?"

"Ten would be enough, sir."

Chapter VIII

Just ten minutes later there was a crisp knock at the door, and upon opening it, Katherine faced a pert young maid bobbing to her. "I'm to take you to Lady Wharton, ma'am."

"I'm ready," Katherine answered and followed her to the main hall. In that ten minutes she had not only smoothed and straightened her gown, recaptured straying locks of hair, but also assessed her situation, calling upon her innate strength to quiet her mind and her emotions. She had not yet decided exactly how she would play her hand, but she refused to be unduly concerned, as she was used to following the flash dictates of her agile mind. So far, she had concluded, she had been lucky enough following her hunches— though, she had admitted the unforeseen presence of his lordship had shaken her and she wished now that she had not been in such an adventuresome mood the night before. Nevertheless what was done was done, and the less time she spent worrying about that, the more energy she would have to apply to the present.

The maid led her down the long hall, which, though dark, was not in the least gloomy. Its walls, lined with lovely landscapes interspersed with delicate tapestries of silk, invited Katherine's interest, but she had to hurry to keep up with the young girl whose slippered feet barely sounded on the highly polished floors as she flew on her way.

The corridor ended in the front entrance hall, which was paneled in rich warm oak. The mahogany staircase, with its heavy column-shaped balusters and intricately carved stairends, faced large double doors now closed to the chilly morning air. Without pausing, the maid sped across the thick carpet, stopped before one of the doors, and knocked sharply.

A soft, melodious voice bade them enter, but the maid bobbed to Katherine once again and slipped quietly away, leaving her to make her entrance alone.

Embracing her wait-and-see attitude, Katherine confidently turned the knob, pushed open the door, and entered. Her first sight was that of a lovely young woman dressed in a pale blue muslin morning gown, reclining on a lounge, her petite round face turned expectantly toward her. Behind her, large lace-curtained glass doors made an appropriate background and frame, completing a delightful picture. Without hesitation the young woman, who Katherine assumed to be Lady Wharton, rose and came to meet her with outstretched hands.

"Do come in, my dear. Lord Milford has told me of your journey. How horrible for you." The smile she gave Katherine was warm and friendly, and the deep-blue eyes expressed sincere concern.

A pang of conscience tweaked Katherine. She had felt no qualms at misleading the arrogant Lord Milford, but she would have preferred to be honest and straightforward with this gracious young woman who welcomed her. With this thought uppermost in her mind, she answered in her own natural, somewhat husky voice—without a trace of the nasal accent of the country-bred miss that she had been imitating.

"Really it wasn't such a trial and the night at that lovely inn was quite pleasant. In fact I rather enjoyed myself." Slyly she stole a quick glance at his lordship, who sat stiffly in a nearby chair, and noted with satisfaction the startled look upon his face.

"I'm truly glad. Charity and James do have an extraordinary place there. When you didn't arrive last evening, I became a little worried—that is until the lad from the inn brought Gerry's message."

Now it was Katherine's turn to be surprised. In sending such a message to his sister, Lord Milford had shown a sense of consideration that she had not expected of him.

As Lady Wharton spoke she indicated a chair for Katherine, and then she returned gracefully to her position on the lounge so they could converse comfortably.

"I must admit, however, that I would have preferred to travel by any other means, no matter how formidable, than be driven by my brother. I can't abide the speed he deems necessary." The brief warm smile exchanged between the two showed Katherine the genuine affection they held for each other.

"In any event, Miss Allen," she continued, again turning to Katherine, "you are here now, safe and sound."

"But, milady, I'm not Miss Allen, I—"

"Not Miss Allen?" Frowning, Lady Wharton turned

to Lord Milford, who had by now overcome his initial surprise and was lounging comfortably in his chair, speculatively watching the two young ladies. "You said that Miss Allen had arrived."

"Not quite. I merely said that the governess had arrived. I made no mention of names."

"Please, Lady Wharton, let me explain," Katherine quickly interceded.

"Yes, please do." There was no anger or suspicion in Lady Wharton's voice, just a questioning confusion.

Katherine then calmly proceeded to relate her carefully planned subterfuge. "Patience Allen, the governess whom you hired, is my cousin and had stopped to visit me on her way here. As she was leaving the house where I am employed, she met with an accident that my mistress felt she had been mostly to blame . . . so she took Patience into her own care."

"Very commendable." Lady Wharton nodded in approval.

"Yes, milady. She is a very understanding and generous person. That is why, when she learned of Patience's fear of losing her new post here with you because of the accident, she sent me to fulfill her duties until Patience was well enough to take them on herself."

Dipping into her reticule, Katherine pulled out the letter of explanation and introduction. "Here is a letter from my mistress that expresses her concern," she continued, offering the missive to Lady Wharton with a furtive glance at Lord Milford. Katherine settled back more confidently when he showed no interest in the letter.

"Your mistress is Miss Kather—"

"Yes, milady, but you probably do not know her, as she is seldom away from Devon," Katherine quickly interrupted before a family name could be voiced.

"No, I have never met her, but I have had very favorable reports of her from friends of mine. It is said that she is an exceptionally capable woman. Did she not take over her father's estate upon his death, including the responsibility of three younger children?"

Katherine flushed with pleasure at these unexpected compliments, but remembering the part she played, she merely replied, "That's right, milady. But she does not mind. She loves her sisters and brother very much."

"And I see she has a very loyal servant in you," Lady Wharton commended.

"I trust so, madam." Katherine lowered her eyes in compliance with her position.

Seemingly satisfied with the contents of the letter, Lady Wharton laid it aside and turned her full attention again to Katherine. "How long will it be before Miss Allen will be able to take charge of her duties here?"

"The doctor was not sure, but if there are no head injuries, and he thought not, she has only to wait until a sprained ankle is mended."

"Probably at least a week." Lady Wharton pursed her lips in thought. After a few moments reflection she resumed. "Ordinarily, for such a short time, I would not have need of her generous offer, but since I was expecting Miss Allen, I have made a number of engagements that I would be hard put to break . . . in fact I really do not wish to. So I will accept your assistance and turn my two offspring over into your charge."

As if on cue, the glass doors behind Lady Wharton were thrown open and two young boys, one about six and the other several years younger, came tumbling breathlessly into the room.

"Mother, Mother," the elder called between gasps, "look what—" He stopped abruptly as he caught sight of Katherine and stiffened, hastily putting his hands behind him. His high, childish voice took on a formal, stilted accent as he apologized. "I am sorry, I did not know you had visitors."

Katherine smiled at the young boy in total approval of what she saw. He remembered his manners, but there was a mischievous glint in his eyes that bespoke of uninhibited boyishness beneath his civilized exterior.

"Yes, Roger, but not exactly a visitor," said Lord Milford. "This is Miss Bottomsly who will act as your governess until Miss Allen arrives," he placidly explained.

Until then he had sat quietly by, taking no part in the conversation between the two females. Who his sister hired as governess for her sons was no concern of his, but the young woman now seated opposite her was another matter. Behind a facade of languid indifference, his lordship had intently watched her, listening to her soft, husky voice calmly explain her situation.

Before Roger could acknowledge his lordship's introduction, Lady Wharton interrupted, again in some confusion.

"Miss Bottomsly? I thought your name was Miss

Hatfield—Betsy Hatfield," she stated, looking down at the letter she had retrieved from the table beside her.

Momentarily Katherine's heart plunged. There was a sinking feeling in her stomach. In her anxiety to keep the name of Tarkington from Lord Milford, she had completely forgotten that she had used Betsy's name in her letter of introduction. She could only hope for the best.

Her appearance showed no outward concern as she blithely replied, "It is, milady, Betsy Hatfield." Then, though not looking at him, Katherine indicated Lord Milford. "When the innkeeper's wife introduced me to Lord Milford last evening to beg him to allow me to dry myself by his fire, she called me by that name. She must have felt we were imposing on milord's good nature, and she evidently wanted him to feel that I was known to her—not a complete stranger, so to speak. I don't know why she chose that name, but I didn't feel it wise to contradict her under the circumstances, since I never expected to see the gentleman again."

"Oh, how like Charity . . . always ready to lend aid to someone in distress." Lady Wharton laughed, accepting Katherine's explanation readily. "And if I recall correctly, Bottomsly was her family name. That's why it must have come so easily to her lips."

Katherine knew there were other reasons but only smiled in agreement, all the while wondering if Lord Milford would give any thought to her apparent familiarity with the name and the stories with which she had regaled him the night before.

If that segment of their conversation had been evoked in his lordship's mind, he displayed no evidence of it, for he gave his full attention to his two nephews, who during the exchange of words had been regarding Katherine curiously but respectfully.

"Welcome your new governess," Lord Milford admonished sternly.

The older boy did not move but stood with obvious restraint, his hand still behind his back. He replied dutifully, "How do you do, Miss Hatfield?"

The younger one, about three, just grinned shyly.

"How do you do?" replied Katherine formally as she held out her hand. Her eyes shone with a merry twinkle as she was spontaneously warmed by the lovableness of the little one and the dignity of the elder—a dignity that did little to belie the mischievous glint still flickering in his eyes.

"Roger, your manners. Aren't you going to take Miss Hatfield's hand?" Though he had posed a question, his lordship was obviously giving a command with which, from the tone of his voice, he expected instant compliance.

"Begging your pardon, but no" was the child's quivering answer.

Wishing to put the children at ease, they were so young, Katherine withdrew her hand and started to protest Lord Milford's command, but held her tongue as she watched the boy's eyes. They grew brighter. What deviltry was he planning? she wondered. An instinct sharpened by close association with her own younger brother warned her to be wary.

A quick glance at Lord Milford's frowning face and a decision was made. The youngster darted forward. "But I do have a gift for her." He unceremoniously dumped a huge gray-green frog on her lap.

"Roger!" Lady Wharton's voice was sharp in reproof.

Katherine, on the other hand, without surprise or dismay, grasped the amphibian firmly in her hands before it could leap away.

"Thank you, Roger. A fine, big fellow he is too."

At first a cloud of disappointment descended on Roger's face, but when he saw the amusement and understanding in Katherine's expression, he grinned sheepishly in response. A sudden, mutual bond had sprung up between them.

Before Lord Milford or Roger's mother could protest his behavior, Katherine had taken control of the situation without their even being aware of it.

"But, Roger, as splendid as this gift is, I can't accept it. A frog must live in water. I suggest that you take him back where you found him." Then, remembering a trick her brother had taught her, she continued, "Look, he's trembling. He must be frightened. Let's put him to sleep, so when he's safely back home, he'll wake up and think he just had a bad dream."

"Do frawgs dream?" the younger one, who had now joined his brother at her knee, asked earnestly.

"Of course not," Roger answered with the superiority of age.

"Just to make sure, we'll put him to sleep anyway."

Two pairs of fascinated eyes watched as Katherine turned the frog on its back and gripped it firmly, gently stroking its underside until it became limp as if lost in deep, unconscious slumber. Quite in awe, the two boys stared at her.

"Now take him back," she commanded gently. "He's a very useful fellow in his own way. We don't want any harm to come to him. No self-respecting pond should be without its quota of frogs."

Roger dutifully took the reptile in his two small hands, careful not to disturb it. Without a glance at either of the other occupants of the room, he scampered out the door, his younger brother tagging after him.

"Miss Hatfield, I must say you have a way with boys." Lady Wharton's amused eyes met Katherine's in friendly admiration.

"I've had a long association with them," replied Katherine, thankful for Lady Wharton's approval. She ignored the strange expression of indecision on Lord Milford's face.

Abruptly Lord Milford arose. "If you two will excuse me, I have urgent affairs to attend to. It seems that all is well here."

"Yes, everything is under control, Gerry," Lady Wharton answered, seemingly very satisfied with the outcome of the morning's interview. "I know Grant is extremely anxious to see you about the mare and her new foal. He's worried about the disease spreading."

So that's why he's not in Oxford, thought Katherine—*a crisis in the stables.* She wondered just what his feelings for Gwen were. It seemed his horses were more important.

After his lordship's departure Katherine's duties were discussed. It was decided that since she was to be there for such a short stay no formal schooling would be undertaken. She would spend her time with the boys, giving Lady Wharton the freedom she needed to attend to her activities. Katherine was to have the room across the hall from her charges and would take her meals with the family. Even little Charles ate with the adults when there were no guests.

It was midmorning when Lady Wharton rang for the maid to escort Katherine to her room.

"Take the rest of the morning to unpack and make yourself comfortable. After lunch, while Charles is napping, Roger can show you around the gardens." With the arrival of the same pert young lass that had first guided her, Katherine was dismissed.

Chapter IX

"Your things are in your room now," the maid informed her as she led the way across the front entryway and up the stairs to the second floor. "Your room is at the end of the hall. Milord's and Lady Wharton's are in the other wing."

As before, her small slippered feet danced quickly along and her tongue kept pace as she continued to point out various items of interest. Katherine listened with amusement. How proud this young maid was of her association with Milford Hall.

"You must like it here," Katherine interposed as the maid paused for breath.

"Cum, that I do! 'Tis the best place to be for miles around . . . in fact, I imagine, anywhere. You'll like it here too, miss. They treat you fine and milord won't allow no bullying among the help either. Each one has his own job to do, he says, and if you does it well, you'll be treated in kind."

As she followed close behind the young girl Katherine wondered if there were any other reasons besides his lordship's fairness that might account for her satisfaction with her situation. She was certainly a taking little thing. Did his lordship perhaps have a penchant for pert young serving lasses? After all, he had shown an active interest in a governess. But really now, she chided herself, she was being unfair. This maid was barely more than a child and Lord Milford did not seem to be the type to take such an interest in children—but then Gwen was barely more than a child.

Katherine's speculations ceased when the girl reached the last room and indicated it was hers. She was delighted with it. It was larger than the first one she had used as well as lighter and airier. A small bed, wardrobe, writing desk, commode, and several chairs, all of substantial quality, made up the furnishings. There was ample space to move about, a soft carpeted floor, and rose-hued wall hangings enhanced the aura of warmth and comfort. A fine, copious fireplace dominated one wall, but it was the large double windows that offered a view of the side gardens that appealed most to Katherine. She would never feel cooped up in here. Then she smiled to herself—why worry about it, as she was only going to be here a few days, a little over a week at the most.

The maid was just as pleased at Katherine's obvious satisfaction with her room as if she herself were the hostess, as in a way she was, thought Katherine. A satisfied, happy staff always owned the establishment.

Katherine knew that a governess's contact with the servant population was limited, and time was short. She wanted to make the most of this young girl's willing tongue. Though usually she deplored servant gossip and never encouraged it, that was just exactly what she had come to Milford Hall to gather. So without further consideration as to the propriety of her actions, she set about gaining the young maid's confidence. This was an easy task, for she was by nature a friendly, unsuspecting young miss.

After first thanking her for her kindness, Katherine then learned that her name was Penelope, but she was called Penny, and that she had lived in Milford, a small village adjacent to the estate, all her fifteen years. When Penny asked if she might assist her in the unpacking, Katherine gratefully accepted.

Taking her few gowns one by one from her valise, Katherine shook them out and handed them to Penny to be hung in the wardrobe, after first inspecting them for need of pressing.

"I'll do that for you this afternoon, ma'am," Penny offered obligingly. "They ain't very wrinkled. 'Twill only take a few minutes." As she spoke she ran her hands gently over the rich fabrics. "Lordy, these are fine."

"My mistress is very generous too, Penny," Katherine said. "We're both lucky in our situations."

"Your mistress—but ain't you the new governess?" Penny turned a surprised face to her.

Katherine hastened to explain her substitute role.

"That's why you have so few things, then."

Katherine nodded.

"But they're all so fine . . . as fine as Lady Wharton's."

"They all belonged to my mistress once," Katherine commented. And still do, she laughed to herself. "But I am sure Lady Wharton's gowns are much fancier than these."

"Oh, they may have more lace and such, but the fabric's no better. I know. My mother sews for all the ladies hereabouts and she's taught me lots about quality clothes."

"Does your mother sew for Lady Wharton?" asked Katherine, trying to channel the conversation to the occupants of Milford Hall.

"No, she hasn't yet, but she probably will as soon as milady needs a new gown." Noticing the questioning look on Katherine's face, Penny continued, "You wouldn't be knowing, but Lady Wharton and her two sons set down here only 'bout a month ago."

"Oh?" Katherine hoped the intonation of her voice would encourage the maid to continue. It did.

"I really don't know all the details, but anyway, as I hear it, she stayed on at her husband's estate for nigh on a year after he was killed. Then all of a sudden she gathers all her belongings, packs up her two boys, and comes here to her brother."

"That's not too hard to understand. It was probably easier to bear to live with her own brother than accept charity from her in-laws."

"No, that's not it. Everything belongs to Master Roger. He's the heir." She lowered her voice to a more confidential pitch and added, "I do think it had something to do with her two cousins-in-law. They were brought up with her husband—practically like brothers—and they just returned from the service. I hear they both wanted to marry her and she had to get away 'cause she couldn't make up her mind on which one and couldn't stay living in the same house with both of 'em."

Katherine could easily imagine two young men in love with the beautiful young matron, but she felt a rising sense of guilt as she listened to Penny's chatter.

This type of conjecture was not what she was endeavoring to uncover. After all it was Lord Milford that posed the problem to her and her sister's future, not the lovely Lady Wharton.

"I imagine Lord Milford was glad to have his sister join him." Katherine tried to guide the garrulous maid onto the topic more suited to her purpose.

Penny was quiet for a few seconds, pondering the statement, but finally continued with a quick nod of her pretty head. "Yes, I'd say he is now, but I don't think he was so pleased at first. Guess he sort of liked his peace and quiet." She giggled. "You should have seen him with those two boys when they first came. So high in the instep he was. Yet, it didn't take long for them to soften him up, and they simply worship him. You know, miss, he'd make a fine father. He really takes an interest in those two young-uns. He treats them like human beings, not just something to show off and then send away to the back corners of the house."

Katherine understood what Penny meant. She had known many families where the children saw their parents for only a good-morning greeting. The real rearing was left to the nurse, the governess, the tutor. Then she thought of her own family—how close they had been, how many hours she had spent riding beside her father, working next to him in the barns, how warm and affectionate were her relationships with all the others, and how much each one meant to her. Even if she never did marry and have children of her own, she had had the opportunity to love and be loved by her young sisters and brother. But that was all beside the point at this moment.

"If Lord Milford's such a prize, why hasn't some fashionable miss snapped him up?"

"They've tried. Oh, la-de-da, how they've tried!" Penny laughed. "When milord left the service and took over here, there wasn't a female, mother or daughter, for miles around that didn't set her cap for him."

"None was successful, I take it."

"Not even close. Very civil and gallant he was to them all. Lady Wharton says he's too busy with his schools and politics and besides he's got his own ideas on what a wife should be and won't settle for nothing less. And I don't blame him. He's too fine a gentleman to be harried by some flibberty-gibbit."

Well, Gwen was certainly no flibberty-gibbit, Katherine thought to herself. She continued her probing. "You seem to think quite highly of milord."

"Oh, yes, miss, we all do. He's so fair—and kind—and generous. So even-tempered."

"My, my such a man," Katherine teased. "He doesn't sound believable. No faults at all? Hasn't he ever even raised his voice?"

"Not that I—well, once he did." Again Penny's tone became more confiding as she slowly closed a drawer to the dresser and turned to Katherine. "That was the time Lord Northup brought the sheriff and took Tom away—accused him of poaching, he did. Milord nearly burst, he was so mad. 'He's got no right to come on my land and take my man,' he says. Lord Northup's a duke too, but that didn't bother milord. 'I don't care if he was the king,' he says and goes and brings Tom back, giving Lord Northup the biggest setdown—right to his face, he did."

Another example of the conquering hero, thought Katherine. Yet she could well imagine that proud, arrogant man defending down to the last inch what he felt were his rights. It was more difficult to picture him from what she herself had seen so far as the conscientious master of the manor or the concerned, loving father. But, then, that's what she was here for—to learn about the real person from his servants.

Suddenly Penny's hand flew to her mouth in a gesture of dismay. "Lum, I've talked too much as usual. It's way past time I was in the kitchen."

Katherine agreed that they had taken an extraordinarily long time to unpack her few belongings. What she could have done in ten minutes by herself must have taken them almost half an hour—but possibly a very profitable half hour.

"I'm truly sorry, Penny. I hope my keeping you here won't get you into any trouble."

"No matter, ma'am." With a bright twinkle in her eyes she added, "I'll take extra pains with the cleaning up an' cook will forget I was a wee late." Quickly dancing to the door, she called back as she left the room, "I'll pick up your gowns and press 'em this afternoon."

"Thank you, Penny. You've been so helpful," Katherine replied, but she doubted that the swiftly retreating figure had heard her.

Or had she been so helpful? Katherine began to wonder at her own reactions as she reflected over all that the friendly little maid had said about her master. Everything, but everything, placed the gentleman in such an admirable light! Why did this nagging feeling persist? Was it doubt? Disappointment? Was she looking for reasons why Gwen should not marry Lord Milford?

The first couple of days Katherine saw little of Lord Milford. He spent most all of his time in the stables. Lady Wharton explained that his absence was due to some trouble with his horses. Why, he had even returned from London at the groom's report that one of his prize mares had died from some disease or other and possibly his other animals were being threatened. From this, Katherine surmised that she had been right—his horses were more important to him than the prospects of finding a wife. Or was he so arrogant that he felt it didn't matter how he pressed his suit, any female was his for only the asking?

But the two boys, eager to make friends with their new governess, took up her time and energy. Bright, active youngsters could make many demands, but these were demands to which Katherine was more than willing to acquiesce. They got along famously.

From them she soon discovered that Penny had been right about one thing. The boys worshiped their uncle. They constantly plied her with praise of his skills of horsemanship, of his mastery of the art of boxing, his ability to shoot, his deeds of valor in the army. . . . At first she listened avidly, but the praise so sincerely and genuinely given by the elder boy and assiduously adhered to by the younger soon began to cloy. Surely no one man was that wonderful. Then again, the boys were just babies and thus impressionable. In any case, they harped upon traits that didn't particularly interest a lady considering marriage.

On the third day, however, Lord Milford joined

them for the evening meal. The crisis in the stables had been met and conquered. He sat at the head of the table and Lady Wharton at the foot. Roger was seated on one side and Katherine with little Charles under her care on the other. The conversation was just about the same as it had been the two previous evenings. Lady Wharton questioned the boys as to their activities of the day and listened with obvious interest to their answers. This evening Lord Milford, too, listened but said little.

This particular day the three, Katherine and the two boys, had made a rather extensive tour of the estate. It seemed as if they had walked for miles. Roger was depicting the details of the venture when suddenly he turned a serious face to his uncle. "Why do we have so many fallow fields, sir? Miss Hatfield says that we waste many good productive years this way."

"She does, does she?"

"Yes, sir," the youthful voice continued earnestly, not noticing the amusement on Lord Milford's face. "Miss Hatfield says that instead of letting them lie idle we should plant turnips. She says that Lord Townshend had shown the advisability of planting turnips every fourth year ever so long ago. She says we're almost a century behind the times at Milford Hall."

"I see, and Miss Hatfield is, no doubt, an expert on agriculture?" Lord Milford retorted, but his tone was light and teasing.

Katherine stirred uneasily as both turned to her for a possible answer. She gave all her attention to assisting young Charles with his meat and ignored them as casually as she could.

"I don't know about that," Roger finally replied,

"but, sir, what she said made a great deal of sense." He continued to repeat almost verbatim what she had told him about cultivation and crop rotation. What an astute mind he had for one so young, Katherine marveled. Even her brother at Roger's age hadn't known a turnip from a stalk of corn.

"You learned a lot today, it seems, and your teacher certainly sounds like an expert. Tell me, does she have any other innovations we should follow?"

Katherine bristled at the patronizing tone of his words. She certainly would have liked to compare her crops and corresponding account books with his. Then he wouldn't be so smug and superior.

Warming to his subject, Roger plunged ahead, his young mind so engrossed in the topic that he was entirely unaware of the undercurrent of emotions that prevailed. He missed the teasing lights in his uncle's eyes and the flush that slowly colored Katherine's face. She remembered too vividly the last time she and his lordship had held such a discussion and how that one had ended.

"Miss Hatfield says that our sheep are excellent examples of their breed—"

"I'm glad she approves."

"But that—"

"You mean that there is something wrong with our sheep too?"

"Miss Hatfield says—"

"Roger." Lady Wharton's soft voice finally intervened. "I think that's enough. If you gentlemen want to discuss the business of farming, please do it elsewhere, not at the dinner table."

Unlike her young son Lady Wharton had been keenly alert to the tension around them, and though not knowing the cause of Katherine's rising embarrassment, she felt sympathy for her and put an end to the uncomfortable situation.

Immediately Lord Milford offered his apologies and turned the conversation to the coming spring fair in which Lady Wharton was so involved. No longer the center of attention, Katherine threw Lady Wharton a look of gratitude that was answered with a warm smile. Relaxing, they finished their dinner with no additional discomfort.

Chapter X

The sense of ease was not long lasting, for Lord Milford also joined the family in the parlor for the evening. Katherine could not explain why his mere presence put her on edge. Probably her guilty conscience, she thought.

His lordship and Roger immediately took themselves off to a small table in the corner of the room and became involved in a game of chess. Evidently this was a common practice for the two. Lady Wharton had brought her embroidery, and Charlie lay on the rug in front of the fire, going over again the brightly colored pages of his favorite picture book. Katherine, too, picked up a book she had started the evening before. All in all they presented a quiet, peaceful example of a contented family.

Tonight, though, Charles's youthful energies couldn't be contained by his book. After fidgeting before the fire for a while, he finally stood up and tottered toward Katherine. He knew better than to disturb his uncle and brother and could sense that his mother was busy with her sewing. To him, Katherine appeared the one most likely to give him the attention he desired. She had found her book unable to hold her interest and, unaware of her actions had laid her head back against the chair and was studying Lord Milford as he frowned in thought over the chessboard.

Penny was right again, thought Katherine. He certainly looked the part of a good father. Gone was all trace of arrogance from his features. There was warmth and tenderness in his glance at his nephew and an air of relaxed enjoyment about him. Katherine mentally compared this scene to the night she had first met him, even condescending to recall that he had unbent with her and had seemed to enjoy their shared childhood remembrances. She watched his dark head bend close to Roger as he made some teasing remark, and Katherine saw again that dark head bending closer to hers—felt again his lips upon hers and relived that moment of racing pulses and unexplained fear.

As if sensing her eyes upon him, he raised his head and turned toward her. Their eyes met, his still warm with his pleasure in the moment, hers alight with confused emotions. Katherine felt herself growing warm under his continued gaze. She felt the blood rushing to her face, but she couldn't tear her eyes away as a new expression entered his—a look she couldn't describe, one she had never seen before, one that set her pulses racing even faster.

By now Charles had begun his assault and was climbing awkwardly onto her lap. Gratefully and a bit too enthusiastically Katherine turned her attention to him, pulling him up on her knees. She then proceeded to bounce him vigorously, which made him laugh with delight.

"Whoa, now, can't have you getting too excited before bed." She pulled the small child to her, wrapping him in her arms, as if holding him would quiet the upheaval in her breast.

"Katherine," Lady Wharton said, again coming to her rescue. "Why don't you play for us? You do play the harpsichord, don't you?"

"Yes, a little, but not with much proficiency, I'm afraid."

"None of us can make such a claim either, my dear," she replied encouragingly.

Putting Charles down, Katherine went to the harpsichord, sat down, and patted the space beside her on the bench as an invitation for Charles to join her there. Quickly he scrambled up beside her, then sat intently, watching her fingers as they glided over the keys. Katherine had always enjoyed playing, but always left her tutor in despair, for she paid little heed to his demands of position and technique. He had been a cold fish, for whom mechanical correctness carried more weight than the underlying warmth and meaning of the composer's intent. To Katherine music was an expression of emotions, and hers, often under unusually tight control, found escape when she played.

First her fingers picked out the notes of a soft nocturne, a restful, haunting refrain, and quite naturally they slid into her parents' favorite love song. As she played she remembered the happy, uncomplicated days of her early childhood. Her tumultuous emotions subsided, and her peace was restored—for the time being at least.

As she neared the end of the piece small fingers began idly to strike a discordant note or two, and, laughing, Katherine turned to Charles. "Let's play a duet."

"A dooit?" his baby voice questioned.

"Here," she explained, taking his chubby forefinger in hers and placing it gently on a key. "Whenever I point to this finger, press down hard—twice. Like this." He exerted pressure; two sharp notes sounded.

"Now I'll play down here." Her fingers danced over a sprightly tune and paused every now and again to point, at which time Charles gleefully executed his task.

"Wonderful! How talented you are!" Katherine applauded. "Let's do it again. Only this time we'll sing the words. Yours are La la!"

"La, la."

"Right. At the same times you hit the notes. Ready?"

Two bright eyes gleamed their assent.

"That warm May day at the fair, Tra la la. When all the world was there, Tra la la. . . ."

They concluded amidst a burst of giggles and laughter as Charles suddenly stood up on the bench, his short little arms grasping Katherine around the neck in an enthusiastic childish embrace. He threw her a bit off balance, and Katherine's head went back. Again she saw his lordship watching her—with that same disturbing, unreadable expression in his eyes.

Unsteadily Katherine clutched Charles in her arms and rose from the bench. "Milady, I think it's time for this young man to go to bed. He had a long outing today, and I suspect he's tired."

Charles offered no objection, obediently kissed his mother good night, and accepted Katherine's hand to be led off to bed. As she opened the door Katherine heard Roger's exultant cry. "I won, Mother, I won! I beat Uncle Gerry."

Walking down the hall, Katherine heard Lord Milford's laughing reply, "Yes, tonight you did . . . guess I had other things on my mind. Another game? I'll show you a thing or two. I'll even concentrate this time."

What was happening? Katherine felt confused, distressed, and yet strangely elated. How could this arrogant, superior male also be so warm, so gentle, and so completely disquieting? He was courting her sister. He was going to offer for her sister. Trying to control the pounding of her heart, Katherine feared that her plans were not progressing as she had anticipated.

While a very upset Katherine was taking her small charge to bed, back in the parlor an excited young boy was explaining his unexpected victory to his smiling mother while his uncle good-naturedly replaced the men.

"Ready for the beating of your young life, my proud man?" his lordship questioned in a menacing tone.

Roger turned to his uncle and replied respectfully, "Do you mind, sir, if we don't have another game right now? I think I'd like to go up to bed too."

An eyebrow raised in surprise, Lord Milford merely answered pleasantly, "Why of course not. I can beat you another time."

"Thank you, Uncle Gerry . . . and good night, sir. Good night, Mother." He kissed her quickly and, forgetting his dignity, scampered toward the door, remarking over his shoulder as he sped from the room, "Miss Hatfield tells the best stories. . . ."

As she watched his unprecedented exit, Lady Wharton frowned slightly, a worried look on her face. "I do hope Miss Allen isn't delayed too much longer."

"Why? What's wrong? It seems to me that Miss Hatfield has been doing an excellent job," Lord Milford commented.

"That's just it. She's doing too well. The boys have grown attached to her in just a couple of days. The longer she stays, the more difficult it will be for anyone else to step in. I must admit this—our Miss Hatfield is a very remarkable person."

"Yes, very remarkable," his lordship reiterated, his voice soft, almost a whisper.

As if his reply had gone unheard, Lady Wharton continued with her embroidery in silence while Lord Milford stared thoughtfully into the fire. Then with a reflective note in her voice Lady Wharton broke the quiet spell. "Papa married a governess . . . our mother."

"What has that got to do with anything?" was the explosive retort she received.

"Nothing, nothing at all. Just that some governesses are quite exceptional."

Again silence hung heavily over them, and even though Lady Wharton did not raise her eyes from the intricate work she was doing, she could feel his agitation as he poured himself a brandy.

"To do what I want to do, what I feel I have to do, my wife must be acceptable in any and every house across the empire. There can be no doors closed to her for any reason."

"Are you so sure, Gerry, that's such a necessity?"

Lord Milford snorted contemptuously. "Every time

I'm in London, I'm made even more aware of it. Every time I take my seat, I become more positive."

Suddenly Lord Milford stopped his pacing, pulled a chair close to his sister, and sat down. His voice was earnest as he continued. "Father died in poverty, probably way before his time, just because he married beneath him. But he wasn't the only one. So many die too young . . . from starvation, overwork, and worst of all, hopelessness. The poor can't help themselves; everything is stacked against them just because they're born in the wrong bedroom."

With a quick toss of his head he finished his brandy. His eyes had become cold; a sneer was on his face. "Our fellow noblemen—what a laugh! The hypocrites have ground them under their heels for too long."

"Aren't you being a bit unfair, Gerry? There are many fine people among—our class."

"There are some." He shrugged and leaned closer to his sister. "But there are not enough who are willing to become embroiled in politics. That's why we must badger, cajole, plead—twist every selfish interest—to get others to endorse our ideals, even if they don't believe in them. Can you imagine Lady Haverly accepting me at her table, abetting my views, if I wasn't wearing the right coat or if my wife didn't come up to her standards? Yet she's unstinting in her generosity to Methodist's schools."

"You do have a hand in that, don't you? Oh, I suppose you are right, but surely your wishes must be considered too."

"Not really, Pamela—not my personal wants anyway. Times are changing. Society is changing. There are the colonies now. They are offering much. The good, strong young are leaving for a chance at a better life. They should have that opportunity right here." Lord Milford shifted his weight in his chair and clenched his fists, emphasizing his seriousness. "Only those who are responsible for the laws can make changes happen, and a man has to have everything in his favor to buck the powers that are fighting any change. I need every—"

"Please, Gerry," Pamela interrupted, laughing tenderly. "You don't have to preach to me. I'm on your side."

"Sorry, I didn't mean to get carried away," he said apologetically, running his hand through his thick hair, a wry grin twisting his lips. "But when I get to thinking—"

"Well, don't think about it now," she quickly interrupted again. "How's the foal?"

Lord Milford smiled at the abrupt shift in conversation, for he knew that though his sister endorsed his views, she felt little of his intensity. Hers was a gentle nature, and her life evolved around making those about her happy and comfortable. Lord Milford relaxed back in his chair and followed her lead. "He's coming along fine. So are the rest of the horses. We still have no idea of the cause of the trouble though."

"Why don't you ask Miss Hatfield?"

"Maybe I should. She'd probably know." Their eyes met, affection and understanding in their gaze.

Katherine felt relief and disappointment the next day when she learned that Lord Milford had departed, first to see a mare, hoping to replace the one that had died, and then to travel on to London. She had begun to anticipate the excitement she felt whenever she saw him, and those feelings of fear and agitation that swelled within her when he looked at her had added an unfamiliar zest to her life. Yet she also realized that she had a more pressing reason for her disguised presence at Milford Hall.

During the next few days she sought out the various members of the staff and questioned them in what she felt to be a very inconspicuous manner—only showing the natural interest of a new member of the household in the lives of her employers. The task proved to be simple. Everyone was eager to talk about the lord and to sing his praises.

When Roger escorted Katherine through the stables now that all was right there, Grant, the head groom, without any prompting extolled Lord Milford's ability and knowledge of the handling of prime horses. She looked over the fine animals sheltered there and could see the evidence. Although some of his ideas on agriculture were outdated, he definitely was up to the mark in obtaining the best for his stable. His military training had abetted him there, no doubt.

It was the cook though who presented her with the most fascinating pieces of information. She had been at Milford Hall since she first started to work—too many years ago for her to even try to remember. Katherine, having had plenty of practice at placating Charity, had no difficulty in becoming on intimate terms with the estimable Mrs. Ruggers. Katherine had made a practice of joining her for a second cup of coffee in the early morning, her sincere compliments warming the old woman and loosening her tongue.

Mrs. Ruggers told many a tale of the young Richard Milford, the present lord's father—how he had spent most of his lonely young life right here at Milford Hall, his father too taken up with his own wild life to notice him and his mother forced to attend her husband's every whim, seldom allowed to remain with her son for long.

Still Richard had been an easygoing fellow and had found many friends among the local people, treating the butcher's son and the squire's heir with the same natural charm and consideration. Later, when he was sent away to school, he was always at the top of his class. He was the opposite of his father—kind and gentle with no interest in the gaming houses or in the sport of the day. Then he happened to fall in love with a beautiful young governess. His father raged, forbidding the match, but that made no difference; Richard married her anyway. His father, not one to be opposed, swore that his son would never take his rightful place in society, and though he couldn't disinherit him, Richard would never see a penny from his father as long as he lived.

Undaunted, Richard took a position as a schoolmaster. Naturally it didn't pay much, but they made do. For the first few years of their marriage they were wonderfully happy and content. Then the children came. The first child, a son they named Jonathan, was literally stolen from them by Richard's father. The young couple was no match against the grandfather's power and wealth. Then the present lord was born and, a few years later, Lady Pamela. Richard's father was content to have Jonathan, but he remained obstinate and unyielding in his stand. Not a particle of help did he give his own son or other grandchildren.

If it hadn't been for Lady Martha, Richard's mother, there's no telling how their lives would have been, and though she couldn't openly flaunt her husband, she managed somehow to see that Gerald had an education. Lady Martha had been just a naive lass in her teens when Richard had been born and she was completely dominated by her husband. By the time Richard had grown to manhood, she had found many ways to circumvent his orders and saw a great deal of her grandchildren. Gerald was away at school when his mother died, and his father followed in less than a year. Theirs had been a difficult, frustrating existence made tolerable only by the love that they had for each other. At the time of their deaths a stronger and wiser Lady Martha, who for all practical purposes had separated from her husband, took the two orphans under her wing and when the time came purchased a commission in the service for Gerald and saw to Pamela's debut into society.

Old Lord Milford had gone his own extravagant way, taking his grandson Jonathan with him. They were the scandal of London—two of a kind they were, wild and unrestrained. What the old man hadn't taught the young cub he invented for himself and for the amusement of his indulgent grandfather. It was rather ironic that Jonathan was responsible for their deaths. The two of them drove a pair of untried horses at top speed—a bet of some kind or another— and overturned the curricle. They were both killed. All that rightfully would have been Richard's and then Jonathan's, had they lived, now became Gerald's.

Katherine had found this tale absorbing and wondered which of his predecessors the present Lord Milford most resembled—his proud, arrogant grandfather or his gentle sire. She had discovered a bit of both in him.

Chapter XI

The next few days passed quietly and pleasantly for Katherine, but it was with no surprise that late one afternoon while strolling back from a picnic with her young charges she spied a smart coach drawn by two fine bays approaching down the drive and halting before the entrance to Milford Hall. Katherine had recognized the coach at once, also the elderly Sommers, still so capable, handling the reins. It was her own. Miss Allen had arrived, and now she would be able to return to London and to her own identity. For that she would be thankful, but she also felt a pang of regret at leaving Lady Wharton, whom she had grown to admire and respect, and the two boys, whom she had found so easy to love.

The next morning she was on her way to London, a little over a week after her sudden departure. Sitting comfortably in the beautifully fitted interior of the spacious coach, Katherine smiled. She remembered the amazement of the other servants that one's mistress should show so much regard for the comfort of her abigail as to send her own coach and groom.

The smile and memory was short-lived as Katherine evaluated the success of her mission. Had she discovered what she had set out to find? Would Lord Milford be the right husband for Gwen? She had believed that the servants who knew him best would be able to answer that question for her. They had been lavish in their praise of him. She had found nothing that could detract from their recommendations. Truly any woman should be happy as mistress of Milford Hall and wife of its master.

Katherine sighed. Yes, if Gwen wanted to marry Lord Milford, Katherine could think of no reason to disapprove. But for some reason that decision did not satisfy her. It did not relieve the concern she had felt about her sister's future. It brought about a sense of loss, almost of depression. What was the matter with her? After all, she wanted nothing but the best for Gwen, and from all that she had discovered, Lord Milford was far above any man she had ever known.

Upon her arrival at Lady Metcalf's in London, Katherine was immediately greeted by her sister, again her usual gay self, vibrant and eager to dive right into an animated discussion of the past week's events. Gwen had thought nothing amiss at her older sister's masquerade. Nothing Katherine did could ever be considered wrong or even improper. After Katherine had paid her respects to Lady Metcalf, the two ladies retired to her chambers for an intimate coze.

Not even waiting for the maid to leave, Gwen pounced on Katherine, gleefully asking, "And how does the grand mistress of Blue Hills like being a governess?"

"Truthfully," replied Katherine with a teasing smile, "it was much simpler than riding herd over the three of you." She then told her sister of the Lady Wharton's charm and the delight she had found in the two young boys. She described in detail the beauty of Milford Hall, comparing it favorably to Blue Hills, but for some unknown reason she could not bring herself to mention Lord Milford or her unexpected acquaintance with him.

Instead she blithely turned the conversation to Gwen's activities. "I must say," she commented as she critically eyed her sister from head to toe, "you do look more rested and seem to be in better spirits than when I last saw you. How did you fare on your holiday from the London scene?"

"Well . . . I did get enough rest. That's certain. The weekend was a huge success; almost everyone was there. The weather cooperated for a change. We rode and danced and slept and talked . . . and I think Janet's in love."

"Good for her, but"—Katherine hesitated, for though Gwen chattered lightly, there was a reluctance in her tone—"it wasn't up to what you expected, was it?"

With a merry laugh Gwen kissed her sister affectionately on her cheek, and then, in a very unladylike manner, threw herself down on the bed and watched Katherine arrange her belongings on her dressing table. "There's just no keeping anything from you, is there, Katy?"

"I know you too well, my dear. Tell me, what was wrong? I know Lord Milford was not here. Did that disappoint you?"

"You've met him," Gwen squealed with delight. "What do you think? Isn't he handsome?"

"Yes, he is extremely good-looking," Katherine answered somewhat soberly. "We'll discuss our meeting later. You were telling me about your festivities."

"It was nice being with Janet—oh, she has a marvelous home, a castle really—and I didn't mind Lord Milford not being there. It was all the others—and I do mean all of them," she added vehemently.

"The others? I can't believe without Lord Milford around that they didn't dance in attendance to you . . . or is that it? Your vanity is wounded?"

"Heavens, no. I had plenty of attention; too much in some ways."

Gwen lapsed into a thoughtful silence. Katherine moved over to the bed and sat down beside her. Taking her hand gently in hers in a gesture of affection, she waited for Gwen to continue.

"Katy, I just don't understand me," she finally blurted out.

The abruptness of the statement and its seeming irrelevancy startled Katherine into an amused chuckle. "Well, my dear little Gwen, most of us are a mystery to ourselves."

"That may be, but when I first came to London, everything was so exciting, the men so handsome, so charming. Everything was so much fun."

"And now?"

"Now? Well, I do enjoy the dancing, the music, the parties . . . but it's not . . . it's not like it first was."

"Of course not, silly. Nothing's new anymore. The novelty's worn off, that's all. You're becoming a bit more sophisticated."

"Partly, I suppose, but that's not all there is to it. I'm sure I'll never be more than a country girl."

"Tell me, then. What do you think is the trouble?"

Gwen looked at her sister beseechingly. A slight frown of annoyance creased her brow and her eyes clouded with distaste. "Don't the young men have anything more to talk about than the cut of their coats or where they purchase their boots? Don't they have anything better to do than play cards and drink or race their curricles?"

Amused, Katherine pursed her lips as if in concentration. "I imagine some of them do."

"I haven't met one." Her thorough disapproval registered in her tone. "I'm no bluestocking. You, better than anyone, know that, but nothing seems more important to them than how to tie a cravat or what polish to use on their precious boots—unless it's how much money they won or lost at Whites. Lord Milford seems to be the only man around who has some purpose, some interest other than satisfying his own thirst for pleasure."

"But, then, he is somewhat older. . . ." Katherine commented, surprised at the restriction in her throat when she talked about Lord Milford. Gwen seemed to be always coming back to him in her conversation.

Gwen laughed, nodding her head. "True! He's so much more of a real man compared to the others." She paused, as if a new idea had struck her. "Or are the others just mere boys compared to him?"

"How about Lord Leatherton?" Katherine hurriedly intervened. She didn't want to discuss Lord Milford yet. "I remember your saying he was witty and charming and anxious to give Lord Milford a run for his money."

At the mention of Leatherton's name, Gwen withdrew a little from Katherine. When she spoke, her voice became even more filled with distaste. "I thought he was, at first. No, truthfully he really is, but he's also more difficult to keep at arm's length."

"You mean he hasn't behaved properly?" Katherine became alarmed.

"He hasn't been improper exactly, but he does so many little things that I'm not easy with him. He holds me too tightly when we dance. He's too lavish with his compliments, and sometimes when he looks at me, I feel like running away and hiding." She gave a little shudder. "I'd be afraid to be alone with him."

"Maybe he's really in love with you," Katherine murmured softly, remembering how she felt in Lord Milford's presence—the excitement, the fear.

But her little sister gave her a knowing look, and then laughed sharply. "Dear Katy, what I see in his eyes isn't what I call love."

Katherine nodded in understanding. "Can you handle him?" she asked matter-of-factly.

"Yes, I am sure I can. I just don't want to have to."

For a few moments the two young ladies were lost in their own thoughts. Katherine, with mounting excitement, recalled the disturbing expression she had recognized in Lord Milford's eyes. Again came that fear, and now, for the first time, she realized that that fear was not of him but of herself—not that she might not have been able to keep his lordship at a distance, but that she did not want to.

Finally Gwen broke the silence with a sigh. "In any case, Lord Leatherton may have all the polish of the king's silver, but he certainly has little of Lord Milford's gentleness and consideration."

So we're back to Lord Milford again, thought Katherine.

"Have you seen Lord Milford lately?"

"Every day since he's returned from the country," Gwen answered dreamily.

"Oh. Then . . . it's serious."

Gwen looked steadily at her sister, her eyes brightening with anticipation. "I hope so, Katy. I truly hope so. I must be in love with him. Everyone else seems so pitifully inconsequential compared to him. You would give your consent if he should make an offer, wouldn't you?"

Straining to keep her voice noncommittal, Katherine replied, "Yes, of course, if you were sure. I've learned only good about him."

"Thank you, Katy." Gwen's voice was soft and rang with sincerity as she gave Katherine's hand a squeeze. Suddenly with the volatility of her nature, she laughed. "He's not quite perfect though. He does spend too much time on his precious crusades, but as long as he takes me about whenever I want, I'll not complain."

Katherine joined in her laughter, though somewhat hesitantly. "I'm sure you would see to that."

"Oh, which reminds me," said Gwen as she sprang lightly to her feet. "Tomorrow night you are going to the opera."

"To the opera? I would like that. How is it that I am to be so honored?"

"Your first duty as my chaperon, dear sister. I've been a burden to Janet and her mother for the last few nights. Not really a burden. They don't mind. Janet's a wonderful friend and her mother's a dear, but you know what I mean. In any event Lord Milford has invited me to attend the opera with him and Janet has to go to a dinner for some relative, her father's uncle or someone like that. . . ."

As Gwen chattered on, Katherine felt herself grow cold. This was a turn of events she had not considered.

"Oh, how stupid of me!" she cried angrily.

Gwen looked at her in astonishment. "What's wrong?"

Tilting her face toward her sister, Katherine explained, "Lord Milford made my acquaintance as Betsy Hatfield, governess. As you know, he was at Milford Hall for a few of the days I was there. How can I chaperon you as your sister?" she finished with a groan. How could she face him and explain why she, Gwen's sister—mistress of Blue Hills—had been masquerading in his home as a governess?

"How can we tell him that I was checking up on him, spying on him really, before he's made known his intentions toward you? What kind of schemers would he take us for?" For the first time the ramifications of what she had done struck her full force.

Gwen's hand flew to her mouth, but not in dismay, for she had begun to giggle. Katherine flashed her a look of annoyance and then, realizing the ridiculousness of the situation, laughed with her.

"I suppose I will have to remain being Betsy Hatfield for a while longer, Miss Tarkington's faithful and extremely capable abigail."

❋　❋　❋

The next evening as Katherine was finishing her preparations for her first chore as Gwen's chaperon, there came a gentle knock on the door.

"Are you about ready, Katy?" She heard her sister's voice.

"Yes, just about," she answered. "Do come in."

"Oh, Katy, what have you done to your gown?" wailed Gwen in dismay as she caught her first glimpse of her sister.

"Just a few minor alterations," Katherine replied blandly. "I removed the gold trim and the overlays, covered the gold band at the waist with black satin and added this black inlay here at the bodice. As a proper abigail I must show the utmost decorum."

Gwen moaned. "I'm sorry, Katy. It's not fair."

"It's not as bad as all that, is it?"

"No, no, no. It's just I know how dazzling you really are . . . and well . . . your gown is so . . . plain."

"Now, Gwen, I am an abigail, not a lady of fashion," she mocked as she surveyed herself in the mirror.

Gwen came to stand beside her and the reflection showed a study in contrast. Katherine was tall, regal, and although her dress was unadorned and simply cut, it fitted her perfectly, the dark burgundy color adding a rosy glow to her soft white skin. Her thick, dark hair was swept loosely back, twisted into a knot at the nape of her neck and, though devoid of ornaments, shone with a luster all its own. Around her slim neck she wore a simple black velvet band. No, she was not dazzling, but rather elegant and majestic. Any man who took the trouble to look beyond the bright plumage of the others would discover in Katherine a beauty that would haunt many a dream.

As her opposite, Gwen was a picture of youthful loveliness. She sparkled, from the jewels in her intricately coiffured hair piled high on her head to the diamond buckles on her dainty, slippered feet. The sapphire blue of her silk gown was reflected in her laughing eyes, and its snug fit demurely revealed her budding girlish figure.

"No, Katy, it doesn't make any difference what you wear. You always look spectacular." Gwen praised her sister with affection, displaying no hint of jealousy.

"I wouldn't call you exactly dowdy either, my pet." Katherine smiled as she gently put her arm around the younger girl.

"Certainly no one would ever take us for sisters . . . and that's what I wanted to talk to you about. Exactly what should I say to Lord Milford this evening?"

After giving her query a few moments consideration, Katherine replied with a shrug, "Nothing in particular. Keep as much truth in everything you say as possible. The more fabrication we include, the harder it will be to keep everything straight. Let's see now. First, introduce me as Betsy Hatfield. Since he's already met Miss Hatfield, that part should be easy."

"Do I know that—that you've met already?" asked Gwen, listening intently to her instructions.

"Yes, yes, I think it would be best, but since you've been away, you've just become aware of that today. Then, secondly, you'll have to make my—your sister's apologies. Sickness—no. . . . Say an urgent business matter called her away. Since you have so very little knowledge of the business part of the estate, you won't have to explain anything."

"That's sticking to the truth." Gwen laughed gaily, her eyes glowing with the prospect of intrigue. "Katy, I'm so glad you're here. Even a dull evening at the opera is going to be exciting."

"Careful, now," Katherine remonstrated. "Don't slip up and call me Katy. I'm Betsy. . . ."

"I'll remember. How much should I tell him about you . . . Betsy?"

"Don't tell him anything. After all, a lady doesn't usually discuss her abigail with her beau. But if he should ask, just weave Betsy's history in with ours. Don't worry. You'll know what to say."

Again Gwen replied with a merry, conspiratorial laugh. "I hope we don't run into anybody we both know."

"I've thought about that, but I doubt if we will. Anyway, I'll keep in the background. I intend to enjoy the music. I'm not going to socialize."

The distant sound of the knocker echoed through the halls.

With a last slight pat to her hair Katherine turned to Gwen. "That is probably Lord Milford now. Are you ready?"

Gwen nodded, and the two left the room, arm in arm.

As they neared the door to the salon in which the butler, as he had informed them, had installed his lordship, Katherine stepped back and gently pushed Gwen forward. "Remember, I'm Betsy."

With a wrinkle of her pert little nose Gwen nodded, then pushed open the door and entered jauntily, with a bright smile as was her custom. Lord Milford rose immediately and moved toward her, his hand extended to take hers. "You are your usually sparkling, beautiful self tonight, I see." He greeted her gallantly, bringing her fingertips gently to his lips.

"Thank you, milord." Gwen graciously accepted his compliment.

As due her station, Katherine had remained in the background, visible as was proper, but not obtrusively so.

"And is this your sister?" inquired his lordship as he stood erect, relinquishing Gwen's hand and turning toward the figure in the shadows.

"Oh, no, I'm sorry, milord. This is Miss Hatfield. She's our trusted abigail . . . though really she's more like a friend or even a member of the family."

Katherine took a couple of steps forward, dipped slightly, and bowed her head in acknowledgment of the introduction.

"Miss Hatfield!" His lordship repeated the name sharply, complete surprise expressed on his face. Then, quickly masking his puzzlement, he bowed slightly. "It is indeed a pleasure to see you again."

"That's right," Gwen intervened lightly, "you've already met our Betsy, haven't you?"

"Yes, our family has had that pleasure."

"Please remember me to Lady Wharton and the boys when next you see them." Katherine had to exert every bit of her self-control to keep her tones casual, for as their gaze met that pounding of her heart began again, even more tumultuous than before, and she caught a glimpse in his eyes of that same electrifying, disturbing expression.

The maid had entered bearing the young ladies' wraps, and Gwen had turned to accept them, missing the entire exchange though the words had sounded quite polite and formal to her.

"Katherine was called away on some urgent business," she chattered on gaily. "Now don't ask me what business. I wouldn't have the slightest idea. Katy takes care of simply everything. Anyway Betsy has agreed to act as chaperon in her place."

Lord Milford moved to Gwen's side to assist her with her cloak. "It seems Miss Hatfield is quite talented at replacing others," he said.

Gwen frowned slightly, then brightened. "That's right. She was replacing poor Miss Allen when she was at Milford Hall. But you are so correct. There are no limits to her talents. We could never do without her."

With a quick, meaningful glance at Katherine, Lord Milford murmured, "I can readily believe that."

Katherine flushed visibly at his words and tone and, to hide her agitated state of mind, gave her attention to donning her wrap and gloves. This evening was having an ominous beginning. There was absolutely no reason why this man should unnerve her so.

Chapter XII

Katherine's concern soon abated, for after they were settled in Lord Milford's luxurious coach each of the participants fell naturally into his accepted role. Lord Milford was polite and at ease; Gwen, as always, was gay and charming; Katherine remained subdued.

Most of the time Katherine simply watched and listened. His lordship certainly didn't seem the ardent swain. He listened with obvious amusement to Gwen's chatter or recounted entertaining but unimportant happenings of the day's session of Parliament. There was a quiet rapport between the two. When he looked at Gwen, Katherine never once caught the slightest evidence of the emotions she had seen when he looked at her. But she did chance to see a look of adoration in her sister's eyes when she, thinking herself unnoticed, stole a furtive glance at his lordship.

As Katherine observed them the pleasant scenes of the times past, of evenings spent in their father's library floated back to her—evenings when Gwen, perched on the corner of her father's huge desk, had excitedly depicted the day's activities while her father listened with patient, loving interest. The picture before her now embodied all the same elements, but it was Lord Milford, not her father, who was now complacently smiling at her. Well, a deep affectionate understanding was a much firmer basis for a sound marriage than mere physical attraction, Katherine tried to persuade herself.

The evening would have progressed pleasantly enough, though uneventfully, had it not been for the meeting with Lord Leatherton. This unfortunate occurrence came during the first intermission. Lord Milford and Gwen, with Katherine in attendance, were strolling the crowded foyer. Gwen's many admirers rushed to pay court but soon drifted away, quelled by Milford's icy alloofness and the protective, possessive air he assumed as he held Gwen's hand on his arm. He had greeted all most civilly, even courteously, but Katherine saw none of the warmth and friendliness he had exhibited toward his own family at Milford Hall. Here was the arrogant aristocrat she had first encountered. Then he spied one particular man—at which time his eyes lit up with an intensity that surprised Katherine as Milford none too gently made his way toward him.

"Miss Tarkington," Katherine heard him say in a voice filled with admiration, "I'd like you to meet one of the most important men in England."

As they approached the man Katherine surveyed him critically. He was tall, slender, dressed completely in black, relieved only by an immaculate white cravat held in place by a single diamond stickpin. The features of his face, his bald dome, full lips, and firm, round chin were not out of the ordinary, but she was immediately fascinated by the arrogance of his posture, which was enhanced by his piercing eyes that darted and stabbed with an inflexible, contemptuous glare.

"Mr. Canning, I'd like to present Miss Gwen Tarkington. Miss Tarkington, Mr. Canning."

So that is the irascible duelist, thought Katherine. She had been one of the many who had been shocked at the thought of two high governmental officials engaging in such tactics to resolve their differences. Yet Katherine remembered it was Canning's brilliant strategy that had led to the successful seizure of the Danish fleet during the Napoleonic wars and that his ability and patriotism were above question.

Katherine couldn't help but note the parallel between the histories of Canning's and Milford's parentages as she recalled that Canning's father, too, had been disinherited by entering into an unsatisfactory marriage and that, though Canning had been raised in society by a wealthy uncle, he was hated and maligned by the Tory aristocracy—not only for his unfitting origin but for his scathing wit, his sarcastic rebukes, and, possibly most offensive, his liberal policies.

Katherine fell to conjecturing if Lord Milford's association with him could be a key to his antagonism toward the majority of society who were engaged in far more frivolous pursuits.

While they were passing the time with Mr. Canning, Lord Leatherton made his appearance. Upon her very first sight of him Katherine recognized the truth of Gwen's assessment of the elegant, handsome man. Although a few years younger than Lord Milford, he bore himself with even more assurance and arrogance; his eyes shone sardonically, a slight, mirthless smile on his lips, until he spoke to Gwen. Immediately his demeanor became gracious and charming.

Katherine, inconspicuous in the background, noticed that after he had lightly kissed Gwen's hand in greeting, he did not release it, Gwen being put upon to forceably withdraw it. Then, taking advantage of Lord Milford's attention being given to Mr. Canning, he closed in on Gwen, Katherine realized, with all the ease and savoir faire of the skilled hunter. Gwen stiffened as he bent to whisper something in her ear, but easily, gracefully, stepped away, laughing casually at his comment. Yes, little Gwen would be able to handle him, Katherine decided to herself, at least in polite society.

With an enchanting smile at Mr. Canning and an apology for her interruption, Gwen suggested that Lord Milford escort them back to their box. The amicable countenance his lordship had shown to Mr. Canning transformed itself into a hard, cold stare displaying open hostility as he turned his attention to Lord Leatherton. But Leatherton completely ignored it; nothing lessened his composure as he protested gallantly at so sudden a loss of Gwen's lovely presence.

Katherine observed the interplay in fascination. Here was a man, suave, sophisticated, whose manner made it clear he would brook no interference in the advancement of his cause. And he appeared interested in her little sister. He would definitely bear closer scrutiny and further investigation.

Much to Katherine's relief, the next couple of evenings Gwen's activities paralleled those of her friend Janet, and Katherine's presence as chaperon was not required. She took advantage of her free time to keep

Lady Metcalf company, ostensibly to lighten her hours of tiresome restraint, but with an ulterior motive of learning as much as she could about the intriguing Lord Leatherton.

Lady Metcalf, a vigorous, forthright leader of the ton, had at first accepted her unfortunate accident philosophically, but as the days extended into weeks her energetic personality, harnessed by a cumbersome cast that confined her to bed or coach, was sorely tried. She naturally fretted, her temper becoming at times irascible. During the first stages of her confinement, morning visitors were plentiful and frequent, but by now had dwindled, a few attending only to pass on snide bits of gossip. Since Lady Metcalf had no firsthand information of her own, she would have preferred not to hear the malicious views of others.

With Katherine's unexpected companionship Lady Metcalf was obviously pleased and eagerly chatted about anything and anyone. Katherine found no difficulty in leading the conversation to Gwen's activities and a discussion of her successful coming out. It came as no surprise that Lady Metcalf, like everyone else, had nothing but admiration for Lord Milford, though she did broach a facet of the relationship that had not occurred to Katherine. Since she adored her younger sister, admiring her youthful beauty and lack of guile or pretense, she found it easy to imagine anyone falling under her spell. In fact Katherine was a bit indignant when Lady Metcalf made her first pronouncement.

"Gwen is such an adorable child," she said, "but I own she is not the type that I expected to bring Lord Milford up to scratch."

"And why not?" asked Katherine, rushing to her sister's defense. "She certainly doesn't want for beauty, and a sweeter disposition one couldn't find."

"Poof, true, she's all that, but Lord Milford has passed up many a beauty. He seems to me to be too much a man of sense to be caught by a bright bit of muslin."

"Perhaps it's her very brightness that attracts him."

"Possibly, but I had always imagined he would pick someone with—well, let's face it—more sense, more maturity. Gwen certainly would brighten any household, but just how well could she manage it?"

"Gwen is no widgeon. She has plenty of sense, but she is little more than a child."

"Ah, that's just what I mean." Lady Metcalf nodded, as if approving of Katherine's finally grasping her intent. "Lord Milford is more than a mere green lad, and I would have expected him to align himself with a woman of—" Lady Metcalf paused and looked intently at Katherine. "Yes, I could readily perceive his attraction to Gwen's sister."

At this offhanded observation Katherine felt the blood rush to her face as she saw again that disturbing expression in his eyes and felt the tumultuous effect his nearness had on her emotions.

"How absurd." She laughed, straining to be light, casual. "I suppose you feel Gwen would better fit into Lord Leatherton's plans."

"Lord Leatherton! Not if she wanted marriage," she spouted in contempt. Then after a short thoughtful pause Lady Metcalf went on, "But maybe he is ready to settle down. If he were, she certainly is his style."

Lady Metcalf's first heedless retort had confirmed Katherine's opinion of Leatherton, but desiring more knowledge of him, she resumed the trend of conversation. "I understand there is some sort of relationship between Lord Milford and Lord Leatherton."

"They are cousins. In fact Lord Leatherton is next in line to the Milford estate . . . and after him his son . . . as things stand now."

"His son?" This bit of information surprised Katherine.

"That's what I said—his son. He married a Priscilla Brampton, very wealthy, very sickly. Let's see, that must have been about six years ago. She died in childbirth, but their son thrived. He's at one of Leatherton's estates up north. Sir Francis certainly doesn't let fatherhood interfere with his own active search for pleasures."

Katherine nodded understandingly.

"He has everything he needs," Lady Metcalf continued, warming to her subject. "Wealth, property, and an heir. Why should he marry? And I'm sure he's in no way near Dun Street. He may be extravagant, but he's sharp. From what I've heard, he's not one to cross swords with."

After digesting these comments, Katherine commented thoughtfully, "I don't think I like his paying court to Gwen."

"You surely aren't concerned about her falling for him, are you?"

"No, not at all. She doesn't find him attractive in the least, but he's rather aggressive and seems to be inclined to have his own way."

Lady Metcalf laughed derisively. "You've made the proper diagnosis there, and any attempt to put him off would only whet his appetite the more."

"But isn't it unusual for two cousins to vie for the hand of the same young lady?"

"Not those two. They've always been at odds."

"I thought I noticed that there was no love lost," Katherine mused, remembering Lord Milford's hostile glare the night of the opera.

"Not a whit," Lady Metcalf agreed. "The dislike springs from a long association on the opposite sides of almost every issue. Besides, the Leathertons did as much as they could to make Richard Milford's life miserable, poor man. They even tried to block Lord Milford's entry into society after his father and brother died. Leatherton would like nothing better than to get his hands on the Milford estate. But Dame Martha was just a bit too much for him. Her stamp of approval, plus Milford's own military record, made him quite acceptable."

Katherine had learned a great deal from her chit-chat with Lady Metcalf, and none of it had put her at ease. First, the questioning of the reason for Lord Milford's interest in Gwen . . . It really didn't seem reasonable that he could be after her dowry. From all appearances he had plenty of monies of his own, but Katherine had noted that his formal attentiveness toward her sister bore none of the characteristics of a man even remotely in love. And Lord Leatherton . . . just how did he fit in to the picture? Katherine felt besieged with doubts. Was Gwen innocently being involved in a family feud? Katherine sighed, perplexed as to how she could best protect her sister.

Chapter XIII

The next morning the young sisters joined Lady Metcalf at breakfast. The sun, already high in the sky, brightened the day outside, while Gwen's sparkling chatter brightened it within as she recounted an amusing story that Lord Milford had told her about a frivolous discussion that had wasted much time in Parliament the day before. Her apt mimicry of his lordship's stern disapproval, even as he depicted the humorous event, had her listeners laughing gaily in appreciation.

The entrance of the butler with the morning post abruptly ended the recitation, as it included, along with a stack of invitations, bills, and notes of well-wishers, two unexpected letters from Milford Hall—one addressed to Lady Metcalf and the other to Gwen. Consumed with curiosity, Katherine eagerly awaited their perusal of the missives, her eyes darting from one pleased countenance to the other.

"Isn't anyone going to let me know what this is all about?" she finally prodded.

"Lady Wharton has invited Gwen to spend a weekend at Milford Hall to attend a local county fair—some sort of pre-Lenten celebration," Lady Metcalf imparted with a pronounced note of approval. "Things are coming to a head."

Katherine felt a bitter pain in her breast but kept her voice light. "How nice for you, Gwen dear. Does the invitation interest you?"

"Oh goodness, yes," she replied instantly. "She invites you too, Katy. A mischievous twinkle appeared in her eyes as she continued. "But listen to this." She read, "We would also be very pleased, especially Master Roger, if Miss Hatfield could attend with you. Her presence here was a delight to us all, and we would like the pleasure of seeing her again."

"That would be quite a trick," Katherine commented wryly, frowning at her sister's unrestrained laughter.

Feeling that there was something going on of which she had no knowledge, Lady Metcalf intervened sharply, "Miss Hatfield . . . why Miss Hatfield? How did they ever make her acquaintance?"

Pricked by a sense of guilt, Katherine turned to her worthy hostess. "I should have told you before, Lady Metcalf, but I had no idea how involved my little masquerade was going to become." Without further ado she explained the presence of Miss Hatfield at Milford Hall, telling her everything—except what had occurred the night at the inn. That evening held personal memories to be cherished and shared with no one.

Lady Metcalf neither condemned nor condoned her actions, just shook her head in disbelief as she listened to Katherine's tale.

"And now what do you propose to do?"

"Well, I truly don't know," answered Katherine hesitantly, looking at Gwen.

"Don't ask me, dear Katy. You're the one with the

clever ideas." She smiled back teasingly. "I'm sure you'll come up with something."

"Isn't it about time to put an end to the theatricals?" Lady Metcalf asked practically. "You've found out what you wanted to know."

Katherine sat quietly for a moment, pondering her ladyship's recommendation. True, she had gleaned the information she had sought when she had begun the pretense, but now there seemed to be complications. Surely Lady Wharton would understand the reasons for the deception. Still, it would be difficult to explain—to tell them that she had actually spied upon them, questioned their servants. The more she thought about it, the more uncomfortable she became. Her innocent charade was now assuming the proportions of gigantic, underhanded chicanery. Then there was Lord Milford. What would he think of her? Not that that made any real matter, she told herself hurriedly. Would he realize that she had acted to protect her sister, not to make an assessment of his wealth and position? Would he believe the two of them were not just scheming fortune-hunters? No, she couldn't tell them and possibly destroy Gwen's chances. Once he had committed himself, had asked for Gwen's hand, she could make him understand why she had felt such actions necessary.

"Well?" Lady Metcalf's single word brought Katherine from her reflections.

"No, not yet. If Lord Milford doesn't come up to scratch, the sham won't make a particle of difference. If he does offer . . . then there will still be time enough for explanations." There was a finality in her tone that told the others her decision had been made.

"Should I accept Lady Wharton's invitation?" Gwen asked, her placid demeanor indicating her agreeableness to any of Katherine's suggestions.

"Do you want to?"

"Yes, definitely!" Her eyes reflected the delight she always found in something new. "I should love to see Milford Hall. Besides, Janet's so enraptured with her new beau, I feel like an intruder."

"As you wish, my dear. Your faithful abigail will attend you." There was no enthusiasm in Katherine's voice.

The journey to Milford Hall was entirely different for Katherine this time. Traveling in her own comfortable coach over dry, firm roads under clear, sunny skies, the time sped quickly and pleasantly. Gwen, having learned of Charity's proximity to Milford Hall, had demanded that they interrupt the excursion at least long enough for her to greet their old servant. Thus they made a stop at the inn which had become such an important fixture in Katherine's memory. After first fussing like a proud mother hen over two unexpected visitors, Charity immediately reverted to form and began to scold Katherine for her unseemly behavior on her earlier visit. It took some time, but before they took their leave the sisters were able to mollify her and solicit her continued silence. Dusk was just beginning to fall as they drove down the wide tree-lined avenue to the entrance of Milford Hall.

As Sommers lowered the steps for them to descend they were startled at the sudden appearance of a solitary horseman. Gwen, poised at the carriage door, stopped abruptly and watched him dismount and make his way hurriedly to the coach. His handsome face, slightly reddened by the brisk evening air, became more attractive as he smiled a warm welcome to her and offered his hand to assist her.

"You must be the beauteous Miss Tarkington," he greeted her gallantly, his expression showing his appreciation of what he saw.

"Yes, I'm Miss Tarkington," Gwen answered, her pleasant smile mitigating the formality of her words.

"Your servant, ma'am. Welcome to Milford Hall. I'm Philip Wharton, Lady Wharton's cousin." He bowed gracefully. "She told me to be present in time for tea. . . . I'm glad I heeded her." There was laughter in his blue eyes, a charming smile on his face, and a sincerity in his tone and manner that pleased both Gwen and Katherine.

"This is Miss Hatfield. . . ."

"Ah, the inestimable Miss Hatfield. Roger has told me so much about you, I feel I know you already." He interrupted Gwen's introduction as he turned to assist Katherine to the ground. "But I must add," he continued without releasing her hand, "the little scamp never indicated how truly beautiful you were."

Surprised by the unexpected complimentary greeting, Katherine became momentarily flustered but managed to stammer, "Thank you, sir. I am looking forward to being with the boys again."

"And I know how eagerly they are awaiting you."

He bowed again and returned to Gwen, taking her by the arm and escorting her up the wide steps. "We are all so pleased that you decided to come. We weren't sure that country life would entice you away from London."

"I'm delighted to be here. It was so good of Lady Wharton to invite us."

Handing their care over to the waiting butler, Philip bowed his way out. "I have to see to Storm, but I'll join you shortly for tea."

Two pairs of eyes followed the retreating figure as he strode gracefully toward the stable, the buoyant spring of youth in each step. Katherine noted an expression of excited admiration in Gwen's glance that was unusual for her, but then, Katherine thought, Philip did not appear to be the usual man.

They removed their bonnets and gloves and were presenting them to the maid when Lady Wharton swept toward them with a hand outstretched in a warm welcome.

"Miss Tarkington, I'm Lady Wharton and honored to welcome you . . . and Miss Hatfield . . . it was so good of you to come."

The two sisters returned her greeting, Gwen answering her with a warm, friendly smile and Katherine with a nod and a slight curtsy.

"We are so disappointed," Lady Wharton continued, "that your sister was unable to join us also. She certainly must be a busy young woman. Gerry, Lord Milford, says he has not even made her acquaintance yet."

"I will attest to that, Lady Wharton." Gwen laughed as her eyes danced mischievously toward Katherine. "But she did make me promise to extend her apologies again."

"Of course we do understand, but that doesn't lessen our disappointment. But you must be fatigued after such a long journey. Tea is to be served in the drawing room . . . or would you rather go to your rooms first?"

"No, that won't be necessary. We stopped at an adorable little inn not far from here to stretch our aches a bit, but we didn't take refreshments . . . and I am rather in need of some."

"Good, then do join us now." Lady Wharton proceeded to lead them to the salon where Katherine had spent a number of memorable evenings as part of the household.

They had no sooner entered the room when a small figure made a dash toward them. He halted abruptly a few feet in front of Katherine, flustered by his obvious lapse in the self-control required of a young gentleman.

"How do you do, Miss Be—Miss Hatfield?" his youthful, excited voice greeted her stiltedly.

Enthralled by her enthusiastic reception, Katherine felt an almost undeniable urge to gather the young lad into her arms, but she realized that such a display of affection would not be a proper reward for his youthful attempt at dignity and propriety. Instead she bent forward and offered him her hand, her eyes alight with affection. "Roger, how wonderful it is to see you again."

Shyly he took her hand and bowed awkwardly over it.

"Don't you have another present for me?" Katherine whispered, her voice registering deep disappointment.

Roger raised his head in confused surprise.

"Remember, the first time we met you presented me with a wonderful fat frog."

A boyish grin rapidly spread across his face, and the rapport that had grown between them only a few weeks before was reaffirmed.

A muffled gasp of surprise from Gwen snapped Katherine's attention from her reunion with Roger and focused it upon the object of her gaze. Standing by the window, an amused smile curving his lips, was the young gentleman who had escorted them into Milford Hall, his broad shoulders now encased in a smoothly fitting jade velvet coat opened to display a fine cream-colored embroidered vest. A neatly folded cravat lay perfectly under his firm chin. Seen in the illuminating light of the parlor Katherine thought him more handsome than at their first encounter in the dim dusk. But what was he doing here? How had he arrived before them?

He took a few steps forward as Lady Wharton began her introduction.

"Miss Tarkington, I would like you to meet my cousin, Peter Wharton."

"But—but you said your name was Philip," blurted a dismayed Gwen.

"My dear lady, I assure you that I couldn't have told you my name, as I have never had the delight of setting eyes on you before." He spoke pleasantly, his eyes roguishly alight as he bowed over her hesitantly proffered hand.

"Peter"—a stern voice inerrupted them—"are you intimating that our charming guest is prevaricating?"

Instantly all eyes turned toward the sound of the voice. There, nonchalantly leaning against the doorway, was an exact replica of the man introduced as Peter. His stern countenance broke immediately into a wide grin as he met the bewildered expressions of the two newly arrived guests.

He stepped forward quickly, every movement emanating a vitality held in restraint by the commands of decorum. "Sorry to confound you so, Miss Tarkington," he continued, "but you are meeting the Wharton twins."

As Lady Wharton greeted her other cousin, scolding him for being a prankster, Katherine recalled what the pretty little maid Penny had told her—that Lady Wharton had taken up residence at Milford Hall because of the homecoming of her two relatives. Penny had neglected to mention that they were twins. Comparing the two, Katherine could well understand Lady Wharton's dilemma. Both, being almost exact facsimiles, were handsome young men, but now that they were side by side conversing amiably with Lord Milford, who until now had only watched the meeting with amusement, she could detect their subtle differences. These were evident not so much in their physical differences, but in the way they carried themselves and in the force of their personalities. Philip personified action, always moving, always smiling, his eyes lit with a zest for anything to come. Peter exhibited a similar vitality, but he was more sober, more controlled. Smiling to herself, Katherine could not help but wonder to which personality Lady Wharton was more drawn.

Tea was served, accompanied by jellied rolls and fresh strawberry tarts, which quickly disappeared under the onslaught of hearty male appetites. Casual conversation continued until Lady Wharton, after admonishing everyone to be ready for dinner at eight and giving Roger permission to join them, excused herself and guests. Since she was retiring to her own chambers, she escorted Gwen to her room. Katherine, as befitting an abigail, remained with her sister to assist her with her preparations for the evening, secretly delighted, but also a little perturbed, that she too had been included in the invitation to dinner.

Once alone in her room Gwen embraced her sister gaily. "Milford Hall is lovely. It's magnificent, yet homey. It reminds me a great deal of Blue Hills."

"A touch of homesickness," teased Katherine, but she understood how her sister felt. She herself had had the same reaction when she had first come to Milford Hall.

Dropping down on a stool before the fire that had been lit to ward off the chill of the early spring evening, Gwen gazed thoughtfully at its dancing fingers. "Possibly," she answered gravely, considering Katherine's charge of homesickness. "I do love the excitement of the city, but I could never live there permanently. Country living is too much a part of me to give it up entirely. I am so pleased to find that Lord Milford also seems to enjoy a more rustic abode."

As Katherine studied her sister by the fire, a darkness seemed to envelop her. Gwen was finding what Lord Milford had to offer more and more attractive. In an effort to quell her rising dejection Katherine told herself that this was to be expected . . . it was good . . . it was what she wanted. Gwen deserved the best.

Katherine's depression continued to grow at dinner that evening as Lord Milford extended his charm even more graciously toward Gwen. He seemed an entirely different person in his home environment. In spite of her determination Katherine's spirits sunk lower and lower as Gwen responded. Though Peter and Philip divided their attentions gallantly among the three young ladies, it was obvious to Katherine that Peter had eyes only for Lady Wharton. The fact that Philip did not seem to mind in the least being called upon to divert her own attention prompted Katherine to regard him with heartfelt thanks and growing respect. Still, she could not raise her mood to share in their lively, friendly conversation. Even Roger, seated on her left, was unable to dispel her gloom—she only hoped that her appearance gave no evidence of her inner turmoil.

While the ladies were having coffee later in the parlor, Katherine asked to be excused, requesting permission to tuck the young boys into their beds as had been her responsibility before. She did not feel ready to endure an evening watching Lord Milford's advances to Gwen, here in the same room where once she had perceived such a disturbing expression in his eyes when he looked at her.

"Why, of course, my dear." Lady Wharton gave her permission instantly. "I'm sure they would relish that, and I know Miss Allen would not take unkindly to your intentions. She is really a very sweet person."

Thus Katherine was entirely unaware of the events of that evening until Gwen slipped into her room late that night. Katherine had already gone to bed, but sleep had eluded her. Memories of the happy hours she had shared with the two youngsters, intermingled with the face of Lord Milford, had kept her restless and very much awake.

Gwen entered quietly at Katherine's response to her gently tapping and sat down on the edge of her bed. Silvery beams of light from a bright spring moon streamed through the windows and merged with the warm amber glow of embers in the hearth; the soft lights combined and bathed the two women. Gwen spoke first.

"You'll be receiving a letter soon. . . ."

"A letter?"

"Lord Milford made his intentions clear tonight."

Silence.

"He had intended to ask you—that is, my sister—for permission to marry me tonight. But since you weren't here, he did not feel it improper to ask me if I were willing for him to approach you. Since he'll be needed here for some time, he intends to forward a formal written request."

"Is that what you want, Gwen?" Katherine's voice was low as she desperately clung to a last vestige of hope.

"Yes, oh, yes, I am sure now," her sister replied intensely.

"You are in love with him, then?"

"How could I help but be—he's such a fine man, so gentle, so considerate . . . everything a girl could wish for in a husband."

Katherine gathered her in her arms and said nothing, her own turbulent emotions commanding her silence.

Gwen gently broke from her sister's embrace, rose from the bed, and glided to the windows. She studied the moonlight-bathed gardens for a few moments. "It is so beautiful here. I love it already." Then in a determined voice she added, "I'll make him a good wife."

Yes, Katherine thought, she'd make him a very good wife. Gwen was an honest, loyal child and knew her duty. But would she be happy? Katherine tried to dismiss her doubts, wondering if her own desires clouded her outlook for Gwen.

"Dear little sister, let me be the first to wish you every happiness."

Katherine and Gwen returned to London a few days later, having promised Lady Metcalf that their visit would only be a short one, as the two sisters were needed to help in the final preparations for Lady Metcalf's lavish ball. Since her ladyship's accident had prevented her from giving what she considered the proper number of fetes due her young charge, she was making plans for one magnificent festivity to eclipse any given that season. Though she was now feeling almost her old self and able to hobble around with the aid of a walking stick, she still believed herself incapable of supervising the entire production herself.

Katherine was only too happy to leave Milford Hall behind her. Although she had spent most of her time with Roger and Charles, she had been inevitably thrown into contact with Lord Milford. Their closeness had been a strain upon her self-control, particularly since she was positive that he was more than casually aware of her. Hadn't she caught a glimpse of emotion flashing in his eyes when they met unexpectedly in the hall and in the garden? Or had it been a mere reflection of her own feeling?

Chapter XIV

Once back in London the two young ladies were eagerly greeted by Lady Metcalf, for she had missed their pleasant company much more than she had anticipated. Even though her ladyship and the girls' mother had been confidantes in their youth, after their marriages and Lady Alicia's move to Devon they had grown apart. Periodically Lady Metcalf had seen her friend's children but had not really known any one of them until she had consented to sponsor Gwen this season. In a short time her ladyship had become extremely fond of the gay, charming child who was so much like her mother; and when Katherine arrived, Lady Metcalf immediately felt a strong bond of affection for this restrained, competent, yet unpredictable, young woman.

Over coffee the very next morning her ladyship demanded a detailed account of the visit to Milford Hall, to which Gwen responded enthusiastically. She described with particular attention her instant love affair with Milford Hall and the beautiful, peaceful East Anglia countryside in full spring bloom. She laughed gaily as she told of how much they had enjoyed the day at the fair and how similar it was to the many bucolic festivities in Devon. Saving the most important for last, Gwen finally spoke of Lord Milford's intentions and waited expectantly for Lady Metcalf's reaction. She was not disappointed.

Lady Metcalf beamed. "That's incredible news . . . what a victory, my dear!" She was jubilant. Her eyes bright in anticipation, she continued, "We'll announce your betrothal at the ball. What a sensation that will cause! I can visualize it now." Dramatically she extended her arm. "Amidst all the dancing and the music I'll announce a toast—a toast to the future happiness of Lord Milford and his bride-to-be, Miss Gwen Tarkington."

"But, madam, if everyone is dancing, how can they drink a toast?" Gwen jokingly tossed the obstacle in her path, sure that Lady Metcalf's opinion of the importance of the occasion was slightly exaggerated.

"Fiddle-faddle! We'll announce it while refreshments are being served, but—oh, it won't make any difference when we announce the betrothal, it will still be the *coup de maître*."

Gwen, not yet versed in the intricacies of society infighting, didn't comprehend Lady Metcalf's rapture but obligingly nodded in compliance. Katherine simply smiled stiffly, wondering if the ache she felt was evident in her expression.

"Have you set the date of the wedding yet?"

"No, we haven't. Everything is a little indefinite as yet."

"What do you mean 'indefinite'? He's either asked you or he hasn't. You're not just speculating?" Her sharp eyes glared at Gwen.

"No, not exactly. You know how proper he is. Well,

he feels he should ask my guardian first, and that has proved rather difficult. She never seems to be around." Gwen grinned impishly at Katherine. "But he's writing to her."

Quickly Lady Metcalf shifted her gaze to Katherine. "Then you still haven't exposed your masquerade?"

"Not yet. The right opportunity . . . didn't come up."

Lady Metcalf silently sipped her coffee while an amused Katherine watched her, for it was as though she could actually see plan after plan revolving around behind those bright eyes.

Abruptly her ladyship set her cup down, looked from one expectant face to the other, and announced, "I have the perfect solution. Another high point of my festivity will be the introduction of Miss Katherine Tarkington to society. That will force the issue, and I am sure amidst all the commotion we can gloss over that whole affair quite smoothly."

Gwen clapped her hands delightedly, displaying her agreement with this aspect of the planning. "Oh, milady, that would be wonderful! Then Katy will have the chance to have a little pleasure—not to be just chaperoning me around. Maybe she can meet someone suitable too."

"Gwen, don't be so romantic. You know I'm not husband hunting," Katherine answered with a brittle laugh. And how true that last remark was, she thought. Now more than ever before the thought of marrying was repellent to her—since she couldn't marry Lord Milford.

"Now, Katherine, one never knows." Lady Metcalf endorsed the sentiment. "Everyone will be here. All the invitations have been accepted, and there have been some additional requests for visiting relatives and friends. I think there's an Austrian—or is he an Italian?—count, a friend of Lord Heath's . . ."

The next two days passed quickly in a flurry of preparation. Every bit of silver had to be polished, every piece of furniture made to shine. Tradesmen delivering supplies merged with decorators and the scurrying staff. All was a hubbub of activity. The sisters, too, became caught up in the excitement, for they had never before been involved in an entertainment on such a lavish scale. This was the only party Lady Metcalf was to give this season, and she was determined that it be the fete of the year. To recoup her hold on her position as one of the leaders of the ton, she had to present an event so spectacular that her absence from the scene caused by her confinement would be totally forgotten.

Since her ladyship was still partially disabled, a great deal of the supervision fell upon Katherine's shoulders, and for that the young woman was thankful. The more involved she became in the many trivial decisions that had to be made and in the smoothing of ruffled dispositions, the less time she would have to dwell upon her own unhappiness. Yet, even though she worked willingly and tirelessly, every once in a while she had a moment to reflect. All this effort was being expended on her sister's wedding . . . and her own heartbreak.

The day before the ball, while Lady Metcalf and her guests were having a late morning breakfast, the post arrived bringing Lord Milford's letter, the final blow as far as Katherine was concerned. With a forced smile she read the formal, proper prose requesting the hand in marriage of her ward, her sister Gwendolyn. There it was in black and white, all settled.

Almost as if sensing Katherine's feelings, Lady Metcalf took charge of the conversation, dominating the scene with her well-wishing and prophecies of a happy future for the couple.

Katherine, feeling the strain of hiding her true emotions, rose abruptly. "It's such a fine bright day, I'd like to take Victory out for a canter. He hasn't had his usual exercise lately and must be feeling neglected. Everything is under control here now, isn't it, Lady Metcalf?"

"It certainly is, my dear. You've done a splendid job. Yes, yes, do take a breather. A little fresh air can do wonders." Her ladyship gave her consent with an affectionate smile.

Gwen rose too. "Would I hold you back too much, Katy? I'd like a bit of air as well. We've had a busy time these last few days."

Though Katherine had wanted to be alone, there was no way she could deny her sister's request. "Of course, come along, Gwen. I can't race helter-skelter in the park as if I were taking the meadows at Blue Hills."

Once in the park the two rode silently side by side. The air was crisp and fresh and did much to revive Katherine's spirits. She was thankful that Gwen was not inclined to engage in her usual flow of charming chatter. Coming to a straight, wide stretch, Katherine's eyes lit up as she felt Victory's pull at the bit.

"Victory wants his head."

"Don't hold back on my account, Katy. Prince and I are content to just walk along."

Without a parting word Katherine relaxed her firm restraint on the reins. "Go, Victory." She gave the unnecessary command as the great bay leaped forward. So what if it was unseemly for a lady to race down the lane? No one knew her. Besides, the park was practically empty. With no more concern for propriety Katherine gave herself over to the pure enjoyment of the ride.

Some distance away Katherine again tightened her grip, turned Victory, and trotted resignedly back toward Gwen. Momentarily she had dismissed her cares, but it would take more than a brief gallop to entirely restore her normal equanimity. Only a few minutes later she spied her sister seated stiffly astride her mount. Someone on a feisty black stallion was at her side. He had one hand on the pommel of her saddle and was earnestly conversing with her. Katherine urged Victory forward. It would not do for Gwen to be left unchaperoned with him, for Katherine had recognized Lord Leatherton.

Her approach did not in any way impede their conversation. Gwen's voice was raised in indignation. "Lord Leatherton, I am to be betrothed to Lord Milford and no amount of protestation on your part can change that."

The tone, the finality of her statement, had its effect, and the smile disappeared from his face; the gray eyes turned to ice.

"You may be betrothed to Lord Milford, my dearest, but that does not necessarily mean you are going to marry him." With a sudden movement he jerked his mount around, riding away without even an acknowledgment of Katherine's presence.

Openmouthed in amazement, the two stared after his elegant, retreating figure.

"What did he mean by that?" Gwen finally asked, her voice possessing a quiver of anxiety.

"His meaning was obvious, my dear little sister. Just the outburst of a rejected suitor, no more, no less. But I don't think you have anything to worry about. There's little he can do. Somehow I can't consider him a match for Lord Milford." Katherine had spoken reassuringly, but she could not quiet her own uneasiness born of dislike and distrust of the man.

"Of course. You're right. He didn't take too kindly to my good tidings," Gwen replied, her bright smile quickly lighting up her face. Still, the two young ladies rode back to Lady Metcalf's in a subdued and unnaturally quiet manner.

It seemed that every member of society, each decked out in his finest attire, had crowded into Lady Metcalf's spacious halls. The total effect was a riot of color and confusion, amid the sounds of music, babbling voices, and laughter.

Katherine had been apprehensive about her introduction, but no one had remembered the ungainly, young female of five years ago, nor connected the majestically beautiful Miss Katherine Tarkington with the more plainly garbed, demure Miss Hatfield who had accompanied Gwen a few times. As Lady Metcalf had assured her, a person of the lower class was seldom noticed. Thus with ever rising confidence Katherine smiled and curtsied, accepting the welcoming greetings of the ladies and the many gallant compliments of the gentlemen.

The rooms were already well populated when Lady Wharton, flanked by her two cousins, arrived. In response to Lady Metcalf's beckoning, Katherine approached them, determined to set things right, yet unable to entirely squelch her agitation. Nearing them, she heard Lady Wharton make Lord Milford's apologies for being delayed. It so happened that he had met with foul play on his way over. No, he had not been harmed in the slightest, but he did have to return to his quarters to change his attire. So bothersome. No one knew any of the interesting details. At least, thought Katherine, that was one hurdle to be put off until later.

"I have a surprise for you," she next heard Lady Metcalf say as her ladyship smiled mysteriously at her guests.

"Lady Wharton; Messrs. Wharton, Peter, Philip," she continued, speaking crisply as she nodded to each in turn. "May I present Gwen's sister, Miss Katherine Tarkington."

As they turned eagerly to meet the long awaited sister, their smiles froze on their faces as they recognized, instead, the abigail, Miss Betsy Hatfield.

Philip regained his composure first and stepped forward, his eyes sparkling with obvious admiration. "A pleasure, Miss Tarkington." He bowed.

Peter immediately followed suit.

Katherine, inwardly bracing herself, turned to Lady Wharton and smiled gratefully as she met no anger or suspicion in her gaze—only surprise and puzzlement.

"Please, Lady Wharton, may I have a few words with you in private? I feel I must give you an explanation." There was no false humility in her tones, only a frank, straightforward appeal.

"Most assuredly, Miss Tarkington. I must confess I am eager to hear what you have to tell me."

Lady Metcalf bade them use the morning room, assuring them of having privacy there, and then proceeded to sweep the two gentlemen away, relying upon their true good natures to dance with the Hartman sisters so that those poor souls would have at least one exciting moment to remember in connection with this evening.

It had taken a few moments to break away from the gathering, but Katherine and Lady Wharton were soon seated, facing one another on the large divan in the now empty morning room, the door shutting out the gay noises of the guests.

"Well" was all that Lady Wharton said as she leaned back waiting for Katherine to begin; her tone expressed curiosity, not disapproval.

Katherine quickly discarded one beginning after another as she rapidly examined feasible openings that would not be too damaging to her image. She had come to admire and respect Lady Wharton and truly valued her high opinions. Finally, holding her head high, she began, her soft voice a bit defiant. She was not ashamed of what she had done, even though matters had got a bit out of hand.

"I don't know how much you know about our family, but our parents died a few years ago, leaving to me the responsibility of caring for my two younger sisters and brother. Since we have lived our lives in Devon, we have very little familiarity with the ways of London society and a very small knowledge of the people associated with it. When my sister told me that she suspected an offer from Lord Milford, I felt that I should know something about him before giving my permission. There is no male member in the family to undertake this task, and Gwen's happiness is of the first importance to me."

Katherine paused, but Lady Wharton sat patiently, making no comment.

"When Miss Allen's accident occurred, and I did feel that my man was partly to blame, the idea came to me of taking her place. You will agree, won't you"—Katherine relaxed a mite—"that a man's servants know him best? Lord Milford was to be in Oxford, or so we all surmised, and a few days at Milford Hall would give me a fairly good idea of the life my sister could expect. Actually that's all there was to it."

Lady Wharton tilted her head in contemplation. "I really don't see anything too amiss in that. Sounds very reasonable." She smiled that same warm, friendly smile that Katherine had known at Milford Hall. "But, tell me, why did you continue with the pretense?"

"That was Lord Milford's doing." Katherine laughed, relieved and now at ease. Feeling certain that Lady Wharton was sympathetic to her cause, she was able to explain her reasoning behind her further actions. Soon Lady Wharton's hearty laughter had joined hers.

"I seem to recall that Sir Walter Scott had something to say about webs we weave when we start to deceive," her ladyship chided her teasingly.

Katherine could only nod in agreement, thankful that the first part of the ordeal had been so successfully passed, but Lady Wharton reminded her of what was yet to come.

"What do you plan to tell Gerry when he arrives?"

"The truth, of course," Katherine answered simply.

"Hmmmm . . . well, don't be surprised if he doesn't quite see the logic of your actions."

"But why not?" Katherine retorted defensively. "You could easily perceive it."

"Remember I, too, am a woman alone with responsibilities and can very well sympathize with your situation. But men—Lord Milford no exception—take things personally. He will probably be quite affronted by your deception. After all, how could the extremely highly honorable Lord Gerald Milton Rutherford Milford, Earl of Sandwell, be suspect?"

"But we had no knowledge—I never meant to—"

"Of course you didn't! Don't worry about it." Lady Wharton smiled reassuringly as she gently patted her on the arm. "He'll come 'round. He does have some sensibility—for a man, that is."

Katherine responded with a weak smile, again caught up in her own turbulent emotions.

"It's a shame he didn't know about this a long time ago." That last thoughtful comment was uttered quietly under Lady Wharton's breath.

Lost in her own thoughts, Katherine had not heard her. "I'm sorry, Lady Wharton, what was that you said?" Katherine queried, shaking herself out of her own state of contemplation.

"It was nothing," her ladyship hastened to assure Katherine. "But now don't you think we should return to the ball? After all, this is really your first."

Lady Metcalf was in her glory as she surveyed the evening's activities. Still unable to move about easily, she had had a dais built along the side of the dance floor and chairs placed there so that she and her cronies could watch, yet be a part of all the festivities. Her fete was proceeding along as planned. Her two young protégées were quite the expected centers of attraction. With the continued absence of Lord Milford, the handsome young bucks swarmed around Gwen, while Katherine, a stately and elegant contrast to her sister's bubbling exuberance, held court to the more mature, sophisticated element.

Yet, as the hour grew late, Katherine felt an increasing uneasiness—an ache within her that no sincerely paid compliment or flashing glance could subdue. Lord Milford and her sister were soon to be publicly betrothed. Well, that's what they all wanted, wasn't it? Yet she knew that she could not be present when the announcement was being made. Detaching herself as graciously as possible from her circle of admirers, Katherine made her way through the throng of dancers and moved toward the doorway, nodding in answer to all greetings with a fixed smile on her face.

The music stopped and the dancers were retiring from the floor as Katherine took one backward glance before leaving the ballroom. Lady Metcalf could certainly feel triumphant. Her ball had been the success she had hoped for—everyone was there and having a glorious time. What a squeeze it was! She wouldn't be missed, she told herself, feeling just a touch of self-pity. With a brief wave to her sister, whose sparkling eyes she had caught as she was strolling off the floor on the arm of Peter Wharton, Katherine turned to leave the salon.

Abruptly she halted, for there directly in her path was the late-arriving Lord Milford. In his cool, haughty manner he was surveying the ballroom as if in search of someone. Katherine's sudden halt brought his eyes around to her. Their gazes locked. There was instant recognition in his, but also surprise, which rapidly changed to admiration, with an intensity that seemed to transmit sparks of fire. Katherine, breathless, was unable to break the spell, nor did she want to. Her pulse raced; the babbling chatter around her became a distant buzzing in her ears.

Then, as suddenly as it had appeared, the disturbing expression in his eyes was gone, replaced by his usual controlled look of amusement. He stepped toward her and bowed slightly. "Miss Hatfield, how you've changed . . . you never cease to amaze me." Lowering his voice to a whisper, he added, "For tonight are you again the provocative Miss Bottomsly in her true colors?"

So he had remembered that night in the inn. Katherine's heart seemed to sing. "Good evening, Lord Milford," she replied, striving to match his composure. It took every bit of her strength to regain her self-control, to dismiss what she had thought she had read in his eyes.

"I was well aware of your many talents, Miss Hatfield. Still you continue to astound me," his lordship continued as his eyes lingered over every detail of her face, the upward tilt of her chin, the smoothness of her soft shoulders.

"Milord," Katherine began, struggling to keep her voice light, "I have a conf—" But she was unable to finish.

"Ah, Gerald, I see that you have already met the enchanting masquerader," a silky, smooth voice interrupted her.

"Masquerader?"

"Then you don't know. You too have been a victim of her charade . . . quite possibly the cause, I might presume."

Katherine withered at his tone and the insinuating ring to his accompanying laughter.

"Charade?" Lord Milford repeated haughtily, coldly eyeing the interloper, all the contempt that he held for Lord Leatherton clearly visible in his expression.

"Let me have the distinct pleasure of introducing you." Leatherton's eyes flashed maliciously as he proceeded to ignore the iciness of his reception. "Lord Milford, the captivating enchantress, Miss Katherine Tarkington."

If the name had come as a surprise to his lordship, there was no sign as he bowed again to Katherine.

"Miss Tarkington, my pleasure . . . the third personality, no doubt." The coldness that had been in his eyes as he addressed Lord Leatherton was still there as he faced Katherine.

Disappointed that his revelation had so little effect on Lord Milford, Leatherton added, the smile on his face bearing some of the qualities of a sneer, "Did you ever imagine, Gerald, that beneath that plain exterior of Miss Hatfield there existed a ravishing creature such as this? What an ingenious method of protecting her charming young sister she had devised! How many different doors were open to her in her guise as faithful abigail! I daresay she has checked us all out quite thoroughly. . . ." Though his tone was light and teasing, the insinuating remarks stabbbed at Katherine repeatedly.

"I am only too happy to discover that she did not find me wanting," Lord Milford replied and then, with a curt nod to Lord Leatherton and a short apology to Katherine, he withdrew.

Not daring even to glance at Lord Leatherton, Katherine turned her back to him, his derisive chuckles ringing in her ears as she left the salon. Fighting back tears, she went rapidly up the stairs to the privacy of her own room. Once there she flung herself on the bed and gave way to her emotions. She realized now just how deep her love for Lord Milford was . . . and the whole affair was hopeless.

Her sobs did not endure for long, as years of self-discipline and consideration of others did not lend themselves to the indulgence of self-pity. Katherine was well accustomed to the habit of accepting life as it came, adjusting her desires to the dictates of circumstances once her mind was assured that she could not alter them. When, sometime later, she heard a soft knock on her door, her eyes were dry even though her heart was heavy.

"Are you all right, Katy?" Her sister's worried voice sounded through the door.

"Of course I am, Gwen. Do come in. I just developed a headache and thought I'd rest for a few moments. . . ."

As Gwen bustled in she cast a concerned glance at her sister. "A headache. Now, Katy, you never have headaches."

"I never attended such a crowded affair before either," she rallied, smiling slightly. "But I'm up to the mark now. Tell me, how is everything progressing?"

Reassured, Gwen sat down on the edge of the bed. "As predicted, dear sister, as predicted. Lady Metcalf has held the event of the season and is now reigning in heaven."

"And your announcement?"

"That was attended to magnificently. Lord Milford and I are officially and very publicly betrothed." Though Gwen giggled as she made the statement, she glowed with all the exuberant happiness usually connected with such a momentous event. "You should have heard all those overstuffed matrons congratulating Lady Metcalf on pulling off such a catch. It was as if she were the one that was going to marry him. It was priceless."

Katherine had to smile at the picture these words evoked, and she realized that she was going to have to smile a great deal in the days to come. Her duty now lay in assisting Gwen with all the preparations for her marriage to the man she herself loved.

"Have you set the date?"

"Not exactly . . . the first of June or the last of May."

"So soon?" murmured Katherine.

"Lord Milford wants the wedding as soon as possible, but being the perfect gentleman he is, he has left the date up to us. But we must be getting back now. A few of the guests were preparing to leave before I came searching for you and I feel we should put in a last appearance before they all depart."

Katherine nodded in agreement and reluctantly rose from the bed. Looking into the mirror, she patted a few stray hairs into place and noted that except for a strained expression in her eyes no one could tell of the despair and inner turmoil she was experiencing. *And no one ever will,* she told herself determinedly as she joined her sister to bid farewell to their guests.

Chapter XV

Following the ball the two sisters were in constant demand, and Katherine, though not one of the debutantes of the year, was acquiring her own circle of devotees. There was a steady stream of callers every morning. Among them, always arriving with Lord Milford, was Philip Wharton. His vitality, charm, and attentive manner toward Katherine was a balm to her aching heart.

Lord Milford had made peace with Katherine, admitting that Lady Wharton's championing of her cause had made him realize that Katherine's masquerade had been a matter of her sense of responsibility toward her sister. With a warm, teasing grin he had commented that his own sister had made no mention of Miss Bottomsly. It was her reaction to this last reference that firmed Katherine's resolve to keep her distance from his lordship. She stringently avoided any conversation with him and forced herself never to look in his direction, giving her wholehearted attention to whichever gentleman was present—an attitude that had unfortunately awakened many an unfounded hope in several poor admirers' breasts.

One morning Lord Milford and Philip had outstayed even Lord Thurleigh, Katherine's newest and most ardent conquest. After he had finally taken his leave, Lord Milford apologized for prolonging their call, but he did want a word with the sisters in private.

"First," he enumerated, smiling gently at Gwen, "I would like to request that you and your sister take tea tomorrow afternoon with my grandmother. She is very anxious to meet you."

"We would love to," Gwen answered immediately. "We've been eager to meet her too."

"At four, then?"

Gwen looked at Katherine, who gave no sign of dissent, and then nodded their acceptance.

"Second," Lord Milford continued, "is to ask you, on her behalf as well as my own, if you have set the date as yet. Dame Martha feels that her health requires her to retire to Bath well in advance of the heat of the summer, and it seems that it takes her quite a while to prepare for the journey. But she's determined to be here for the ceremony." His lordship chuckled amusedly. "She's been after me to marry for many a year and vows she won't leave London until the knot is tied."

After a little discussion the last day in May was decided upon, a date sufficiently earlier than anyone's plans for departure from London so as not to interfere with them.

The days flew by. Every second seemed to be doubly accounted for. There were such activities as the choosing of fabrics, patterns, and accessories; the tiresome sittings with the dressmaker; and the continuing, never-ending round of parties. After the first of the bans had been posted, congratulations and gifts began to arrive, soon filling the small salon that had been set aside to display them. Lady Metcalf had persuaded the sisters to allow her to oversee the proceeding and to hold the reception in her London home. Arrangements had been made for Agatha and Clifford, the girls' younger siblings, to be escorted to the wedding by their neighbor, who had been so delighted to have a legitimate reason to drag her husband away from the country that she had offered to keep the two children with her during the festivities.

Though Katherine avoided any close contact with Lord Milford, as Gwen's sister and chaperon she often found herself in the same company. She became more and more aware—and highly diverted—by what she termed his dual personality, the formal, haughty Lord Milford whenever they appeared in public and the amused, gallant, though reserved, person he was within their more intimate circle. Not knowing whether she wanted to find them or not, Katherine watched for signs of a more ardent emotion felt by his lordship toward Gwen, but was never able to perceive any. She saw tenderness, concern, consideration, but not, she thought, love.

Fully recognizing the hopelessness of her own situation, Katherine tried to dispel Lord Milford from her heart and mind but was unsuccessful. Whenever her guard was down, his face appeared before her, his voice rang in her ears. If it hadn't been for Philip, she felt she would not have been able to endure the many demands placed upon her. Katherine grew more fond of him each day. His charm and gaiety had a steadying effect upon her. He had not returned to the estate with his brother, having insisted that there was never enough there for two to do. Instead he claimed he could be of more use to Milford, who in turn designated him to be best man.

From Philip, Katherine learned much about the relationship between the two families. Although their estates stretched side by side, their close association had not begun until the elder Wharton was transferred to Milford's command. While on leave Wharton had been invited by Lord Milford—then Major Milford—to spend some time with him at his grandmother's home. There he had met Lady Pamela. They were married a short time later, a perfect match.

Wellington was gathering his men around Brussels in preparation to halt Napoleon's resurgence when Philip and Peter joined their cousin under Milford's command. During those uncertain days a bond of friendship was forged among the four, only to be broken by the tragedy of death. For on that victorious day at Waterloo, Lady Pamela's husband was killed.

Whenever Philip spoke of his former commanding officer, Katherine detected the great admiration and respect the younger man felt for his lordship. It seemed that no matter in what area of endeavor his lordship was engaged, those under his protection looked up to him with almost reverent awe.

One other person's attentions to Gwen were unabated. In fact his presence was more in evidence at every event the sisters attended. Nevertheless Lord Leatherton's attitude had seemingly undergone a change. He was always charming, always endeavoring to be of service, always impressing them with his wit and consideration. Possibly he had realized that his bold advances met only with rebuff and was now changing his tactics. Nothing in his manner or his expression could be censored. Both Gwen and Katherine somewhat mollified their aversion to him.

Therefore it was no surprise when one evening Lord Leatherton was the first to greet them as they arrived at the ball given by the very straitlaced Lady Haverly. Lord Milford had been detained by an urgent message from his grandmother and had insisted that the three go on ahead and make his apologies. Lady Haverly was not one to be slighted or inconvenienced—particularly by Lord Milford.

As usual Katherine was soon surrounded by a bevy of admirers and went gaily from one partner to another. She never allowed herself one moment of respite to reflect on what might have been. Her usual restraint had been cast aside, and she had plunged into the active frivolities of the haut ton wholeheartedly.

Nevertheless, as she danced and flirted, she still kept a watchful eye on her younger sister, more from habit than real concern. This particular evening she felt a rising anxiety, for she had noticed that Gwen was more often in the company of Lord Leatherton than not. Where was Milford? She was positive that Leatherton had stood up with Gwen at least two times already, and the evening was still fairly young. Although Gwen was always bright and cheerful, her light laughter constantly punctuating her conversation, Katherine sensed an unusual abandonment in her manner.

Like most young females Gwen enjoyed the attentions of her many admirers and casually flirted with them, but never before had she overstepped the bounds. When Katherine spied Gwen clinging to Leatherton's arm and provocatively smiling up at him, she decided to intervene.

Unnerved at what she saw, Katherine hastily excused herself and hurried to her sister's side, leaving an amazed young gallant standing alone on the dance floor.

"Gwen, my dear, I've been looking for you." Katherine intruded on the couple's rapt conversation.

At the sound of her voice Gwen turned a dazzling smile and unnaturally bright, dazed eyes to her sister. "Oh, Katy, isn't this the most marvelous ball we've ever attended?" Her voice was high with excitement, and she swayed ever so slightly as Lord Leatherton relaxed his hold around her waist.

"*What is the matter with her?* Katherine asked herself. *She's always distrusted Leatherton and here she is literally hanging on him.* Suddenly realization dawned upon her. Gwen was intoxicated. But how? She never touched anything stronger than a very light wine, and then only a sip or two. In any case nothing stronger than punch was ever served at Lady Haverly's.

"I do trust you are enjoying yourself as much as we, my dear Miss Tarkington." Leatherton's purr put an end to her speculations. "Your sister and I were just going for a stroll in the gardens. Won't you join us?"

Even before Katherine could assent, Leatherton continued, "But no, I see one of your admirers striding forward to claim you. I know you don't wish to disappoint him. You will excuse us, I am sure." He deftly clamped his hand on Gwen's arm to lead her off.

Realizing that she could not allow Gwen to spend any more time with Lord Leatherton in her tipsy condition—or with anyone else for that matter—Katherine groped for a plan of action. She could not cause a scene here by the dance floor.

"Lord Leatherton." Katherine's voice was soft, but cold. "Thank you for seeing that my sister has such an enjoyable evening. I'm sure Lord Milford will appreciate your efforts." Though there was a slight smile on her lips, her gray eyes were ice.

Katherine's intent was not lost on Leatherton, and an easy smile enhanced the glitter of triumph in his eyes as he bowed. "I'm at your ladies' bidding, always."

During the seconds his eyes were not upon her, Katherine inserted one end of her fan in the folds of Gwen's gown so that as she turned away, still clinging to his lordship's arm, there was the sound of ripping fabric.

"Oh, how clumsy of me," Katherine exclaimed, an expression of innocence and horror on her face. "I've caught my fan in your beautiful gown. Gwen, will you ever forgive me? I've torn it!"

Giggling, Gwen released her hold on Leatherton's arm and awkwardly tried to assist Katherine in extricating the offensive object but only succeeded to make matters worse. "Katy, Katy my beautiful gown," she moaned as the fan was finally removed, revealing a jagged tear.

"How careless of me . . . I'm so sorry," Katherine apologized profusely. "But I can mend it. It will take only a few seconds."

Brightening, Gwen commenced to chant in her

sweet singsong voice, "Katy can fix it, Katy can fix it. Katy can do anything."

"Hush, Gwen. Of course I can mend it." Turning to Lord Leatherton, who had helplessly watched the proceedings, his frustration rising, she said, "I'm so sorry this happened, but I'm afraid we'll have to mend her gown before it's made any worse. You will excuse us, just for a few moments, won't you?"

Leatherton started to protest but realized that Katherine had bested him and only nodded. Taking Gwen's hand in his he drew it gently to his lips. "I'll wait breathlessly for your return. Don't let anything keep us apart too long."

Leatherton was laying it on pretty thick. *I wonder what he is up to*, thought Katherine as she drew her sister's arm through hers and led her from the floor. But what was she to do now? She certainly could not seek out Lady Haverly with Gwen in this condition, but she had to secure her somewhere where she wouldn't be noticed. With rising distress, Katherine looked around for a maid, but her search was interrupted by Philip, who came striding up to them. Gwen greeted him with a brilliant smile to which, much to Katherine's surprise, Philip responded with a sudden burst of laughter.

"My God, she's foxed!"

"Is it that evident?" Katherine moaned.

Indignantly Gwen pulled herself erect. "Philip, how could you say such a thing? I've had nothing but a few glasses of that delicious punch. It's just that this is such a wonderful party and I'm having a wonderful time . . . everybody is so wonderful. . . ."

174

Katherine, wincing at the slight slurring she had detected in Gwen's chatter, spoke quietly to Philip. "Get the carriage. Hurry! We must leave now."

Though Katherine spoke softly, Gwen had heard her and turned on her sister petulantly. "No. I don't want to go now. I want some more of that wonderful punch . . . I'm not going to leave this wonder—"

Gently Philip took her hand. "But, Gwen, it's such a beautiful spring night. The air is soft and sweet; the stars are bright. Wouldn't it be more fun to ride in the park?"

Instantly Gwen's displeasure was transformed into excited anticipation. "A ride in the park? At night? How daring! Let's do that. Philip, you do think of such exciting things."

"It will be wonderful." He grinned at her. "By the time you have your wrap, I'll have the carriage at the door."

Philip was as good as his word, for as Katherine was helping Gwen fasten her cloak, he rejoined them and escorted them to the waiting carriage. Katherine entered first, then gave her hand to Gwen who with Philip's assistance was quickly bundled unceremoniously into the carriage. As soon as the footman raised the steps and regained his position, the driver cracked his whip and the horses leaped forward.

Now that the danger of scandal had been averted, Katherine leaned back, emitting a sigh of relief, and was even able to smile as she listened to Gwen's soft voice chanting melodically, "For a ride in the park we will go. My true love and me . . . a riding in the park just we two . . . no, three. . . ."

Then silence. The cool night air and the swaying motion of the coach had taken their effects. Katherine turned to discover Gwen, either sound asleep or passed out, encircled in Philip's protective arms, her golden head on his broad chest.

Philip's eye caught Katherine's, and they glinted merrily. "Looks as if little sister has a lot to learn about the ways of city folk."

"You certainly take this rather lightly, I must say," Katherine admonished.

"What's there to be in a tizz about? Some gay blade spiked the punch." With a chuckle Philip added, "What a conversation piece a brawl at Lady Haverly's would make! Just some prankster's idea of a joke."

"I'm not so sure," Katherine replied thoughtfully. "I had quite a few glasses of that punch. There was nothing intoxicating in it. Did you notice any of the other ladies behaving . . . tipsy?"

"You're sure there was nothing in that punch?"

Katherine nodded.

"You mean to say that you think someone singled out Gwen?" The amusement was now gone from Philip's tone.

"And I think I know who too."

"Francis Leatherton," Philip snorted so abruptly that Gwen stirred uneasily. "But why?"

Remembering that morning in the park and the implications of Leatherton's parting words, she replied, "I think he's attempting to break up Gwen's engagement with Lord Milford—evidently even if he has to damage her character."

"Hmmmm, yes, I can see Gerry taking an exceptionally dim view of his betrothed drunkenly cavorting in

Leatherton's company, particularly at Lady Haverly's."

"Surely," Katherine's voice exploded, "Lord Milford would never suspect Gwen of any impropriety."

"No, no, of course not, but he would be put out somewhat. After all her . . . little indiscretion . . . would have occurred at Lady Haverly's. He'd be sure to frown at any activity that might evoke her censure. He sets a pretty high store on her favor."

"Well, I never suspected the mighty Lord Milford of toadeating," Katherine retorted, her voice dripping with sarcasm.

"Not toadeating, my dear Katherine," Philip explained solemnly, "just politics. Gerry doesn't play at politics—it's a serious business with him. Lady Haverly wields a lot of influence over her husband and he happens to be, right now, a wavering Tory. Besides, Milford would do most anything to keep shekels flowing to the schools."

"Schools?" Such a word foreign to their topic caught Katherine by surprise.

Philip chuckled at her mystification. "That's right, schools. He backs and is forever hounding others to support some of Lord Russell educational endeavors."

"But Lord Russell—he was just a wandering preacher."

"True, but he also believed in education for the poor and had organized a number of schools through his meetings. Milford cares nothing for his religion, but education as a way of bettering oneself has been a fetish with him ever since I've known him. He'd assist the devil himself to advance his cause. And Lady Haverly has been generous in that area, I might add."

The conversation in the inn when she had first heard Lord Milford's name came back to her—now with more meaning. Indeed, thought Katherine, could one ever really know that man? Lord Milford was not a dual personality, but a manysided one, and each new aspect of his character only enhanced the others.

"So Leatherton thought to give Lord Milford cause for concern by putting Gwen down with Lady Haverly?" mused Katherine.

"Could be, but I doubt if Gwen's momentary lack of gentility would be sufficient to cause Gerry much consternation—it certainly would not impede his wedding plans. Just what," Philip continued after a pause, his face darkening, "other intention Leatherton had in mind is the real question. Possibly he meant to—"

"No, even he couldn't be so dastardly," Katherine interrupted, greatly agitated by the thought of what Philip was suggesting.

"Listen, Katherine," Philip's voice was now hard and cold. "Leatherton hates Gerry. There's a long history of animosity between the two branches of that family, and besides, he wants Milford Hall. There's nothing short of murder that Leatherton wouldn't undertake to gain his ends."

"But why does he want Milford Hall? He's not lacking in wealth."

Philip sneered. "He's the type that becomes obsessed with possessions. His only use for money is to beget more. If Gerry dies without issue, Leatherton becomes the master of Milford Hall. I'm not too sure about the details, but once the estate all belonged to Leatherton's grandfather. Francis has always felt he was denied part of his inheritance, but he's never raised any commotion. Since Gerry was single and serving in the army, he was content to bide his time. I guess he counted upon the French to take care of his problem for him. But now . . ."

Katherine's mind was in a turmoil. "What are we to do, then?" she asked, confused as an unnatural feeling of helplessness surged through her. No ideas came to her for the protection of her sister.

"The wedding is less than a week away. There's nothing much we can do but see that Gwen is never out of our sight 'til then," replied Philip.

"Shouldn't we tell Lord Milford of our suspicions?"

"No, I don't think so. As you said, we have only suspicions, and Gerry detests Leatherton enough already without adding more fuel. If we just play the part of watchdogs, everything will be all right." He took Katherine's hand in his own and gave it a reassuring squeeze.

The confidence in his voice, the strength she felt in his grip helped to restore Katherine's aplomb. Surely the two of them could protect Gwen.

Chapter XVI

Calmed by Philip's confident, reassuring words, Katherine allowed her mind to dwell on all that he had told her about his lordship. Although she tried to consider only his more noble traits—she found herself continually envisioning his handsome face, his eyes alight with desire as he bent to kiss her. That was so long ago, that night in the inn.

Lost in her reverie, she was startled when the carriage come to a halt before the entrance to Lady Metcalf's home—even more surprised at the blaze of lights and the sounds of music that drifted from the open window.

"La, Philip, I had forgotten. Lady Metcalf is holding a musicale tonight."

Sizing up the situation, Philip leaned out the window and calmly instructed the driver to take them around to the servants' entrance. When he again pulled the horses to a standstill, Katherine and Philip tried in vain to revive Gwen, who obstinately refused to join them from her stupor. Grinning, Philip finally admitted defeat and nimbly jumped from the carriage. Katherine half lifted, half pushed Gwen into his waiting arms.

The footman, his face as impassive as if this type of debauching was an everyday occurrence, then lowered the steps and gave his hand to assist Katherine. *I wonder just what they'll be saying in the servants' quarters,* Katherine mused as she smiled her thanks to the stoic servant, and then turned to join the others who had gone on ahead.

Katherine followed them into the building, thankful that Lady Metcalf's musicale had kept the servants busy and that they encountered no one in the halls. Philip carried his still sleeping burden up the wide staircase and, following Katherine's lead, entered her room and gently deposited Gwen on the bed.

Straightening up, he turned to Katherine with a sly grin. "I hope she doesn't suffer too much tomorrow."

In spite of herself Katherine smiled in return. "It's all part of growing up in our sinful society, I guess." Then, after she rang for Betsy, she continued, "I'll meet you downstairs in a few minutes." Philip left, still grinning

When Katherine did finally join him at the entryway at the foot of the stairs, she found him deep in conversation with Lord Milford. Her surprise at seeing him was accentuated by the usual quickening of her pulse that seemed to accompany their every meeting—a physical state that Katherine had tried in vain to control.

As she approached, her composure showing none of the turbulence she felt, Philip hastened to explain. "Gerry just arrived and I've been admonishing him to give his bride-to-be a little time to rest. I told him she was even too tired to stay at tonight's ball."

Taking her cue, Katherine soothed away the concerned expression from Lord Milford's face and added that a good night's rest would be sufficient for recuperation. As was her usual habit, Katherine began to make her own excuses for an early departure. The less she saw of Lord Milford, the more easily her own life ran, but much to her dismay before she was able to formulate a proper exit line, she was interrupted by the sounds of polite applause, the opening of doors, and the rising tones of chatter and laughter. Lady Metcalf's musicale was over, and the guests were entering the hall on their way to the salon, where the refreshment tables had been stacked with delicacies. At their forefront was Lady Metcalf, leaning, now ever so lightly, on her cane.

"Why," she cried out in alarm as she discovered them, "you're so early. Nothing's wrong?"

"No, no, nothing, Lady Metcalf, except fatigue." Katherine was quick to reassure her.

Then with a knowing nod her ladyship added, "And I suspect not too lively an affair."

Pushing to the back of her mind a picture of Gwen's vivid smile and intoxicated behavior, Katherine shrugged and murmured, "Well, you know—"

"Indeed, I do. But come, you will join us for a little refreshment before you retire." Her glance commanded all three.

Again before Katherine was able to refuse, Lord Milford accepted heartily. "Thank you, gracious lady. I've missed my dinner tonight and am truly ravenous."

"Good, good," her ladyship responded halfheartedly, her attention diverted elsewhere. Quickly taking Philip by the arm, she coaxed, "Come with me, Philip. There's someone I'd like you to meet, a lovely girl, the daughter of a dear friend." Philip was too much the gentlemen to protest.

Somewhat stiffly Lord Milford offered Katherine his arm, and she hesitantly placed her fingers lightly on it. Together they walked silently into the salon. Her serene composure completely masked her racing heart. To escape now would seem unwarrantably rude.

After filling their plates, Lord Milford led her to a table set apart form the rest and immediately upon being seated began to devour his food. Katherine daintily picked at hers. With amusement she watched him, as he took little note of the artistically decorated dainties, stowing away an abundant amount. "You certainly must have been busy to have put off dining for so long," she commented wryly.

His lordship's hand stopped suddenly midway between plate and mouth. A rather self-conscious smile turned the corners of his mouth. Katherine's heart quivered. There wasn't a trace of arrogance in his expression. Why, he even looked boyish.

"Busy is not quite the word for it, Miss Tarkington." He continued eating.

They sat in silence for a while. His slight smile had vanished, replaced by a puzzled frown. Though Katherine was conscious of a dull ache within her breast, she felt a bittersweet contentment just sitting across from him. She felt no need for idle conversation, no need to impress or forestall him. It was both wonderful and heart-rending to be so near him.

Shoving his plate aside, his appetite apparently assuaged, Lord Milford leaned back in his chair, still lost in his own reflections. Finally he spoke. His voice was calm, but there were creases of a frown between his brows. "Did everything go well at Lady Haverly's ball?"

Taken aback by his unexpected question and a bit suspicious, wondering if he had already been told of Gwen's unusual behavior, Katherine paried, "Well? Just what do you mean?"

"Nothing in particular. Did you have a good time?" His tone was noncommittal.

"Why, yes. Yes, of course. Why shouldn't we have?"

"You left so early."

Katherine could read nothing by his expression. Evidently he had stopped by Lady Haverly's to join them and been told of their sudden departure. Had someone commented on Gwen's gaiety or Leatherton's attentions? Had Lord Leatherton himself purposely dropped some malicious insinuations? Katherine was tempted to tell him the truth, the entire truth, of Leatherton's remarks during their meeting in the park and of the unsettling events of this evening, but heeding Philip's decision, she proceeded to explain without divulging all the details.

"Well, to tell the truth, Gwen wasn't feeling too well," she drawled as she contemplated just how to word her revelations. Then, her decision made, she smiled knowingly. "Yes, I guess I had better tell you the truth. You might form the wrong impression if you heard it from someone else."

Instantly Lord Milford was alert.

"Someone—Philip thought one of the young bucks— just as a practical joke, you know, added some liquor to the punch. And Gwen . . . well, she's not accustomed to it and felt its effects—rather obviously, I might add."

His lordship frowned sternly.

"Oh, she behaved perfectly. She's so lively naturally, I don't believe anyone else really noticed anything. Philip and I persuaded her to leave in plenty of time to avoid—well, to avoid any scandal." Katherine had kept her voice light and now laughed easily. "But she certainly was an exceptionally happy little girl."

With that explanation Lord Milford relaxed, his eyes twinkling. "I hope she will be in the morning."

"Philip made a similar comment."

"I must apologize for not being there to attend her. I should have very much liked to have had the company of an even gayer Gwen, but. . . ." His face clouded.

Concerned by the sudden change in his attitude, Katherine questioned, "Did something go amiss, milord?"

"I'm not sure. Yes, something did go wrong. I was sent on a wild goose chase to the country, my horse stolen, and, if I hadn't been lucky enough to come upon an old farmer bringing home a stray cow, I'd still be wandering the byways."

So, thought Katherine, the whole evening had been well planned. Lord Leatherton had been thorough. Again she toyed with the idea of revealing her suspicions to him, but her thoughts were interrupted by his lordship's dismissal of the subject.

"It seems there were two jokers loose tonight." Katherine felt rather than heard a softer, gentler note in his voice as he continued. "Speaking of jokers. There is something else that keeps puzzling me."

"Oh?"

"I can sympathize with the Miss Hatfield charade, but I still don't understand why Miss Bottomsly."

Katherine trembled slightly—they were treading on dangerous ground. She forced herself to laugh lightly.

"Oh, Miss Bottomsly—she was born on the spur of the moment."

A quizzical, amused expression on Lord Milford's face prompted Katherine to continue, "Well, if you could have seen yourself, milord, so arrogant, so self-centered, so insensitive to another's misfortune. I just wanted to annoy you a little bit." Finishing her explanation, Katherine raised her eyes to his.

The prim, satisfied smile on her face became a fixed expression as her blood began to race and her whole body tingled. Exerting every effort, she tried to break the spell that locked their gaze, but in vain. Slowly his hand reached across the table and covered hers. His fingers tightened around her in a painful grip of steel. Still, she didn't try to pull away. The lights in his eyes were no longer sparks of amusement but intense fires of desire. Katherine knew her own were telling him all she had fought to hide for so long.

"And that you did," he spoke huskily. "Miss Bottomsly has annoyed, tormented, and practically driven me out of my mind."

No, no, he wasn't saying those things. It was just another one of her fantasies, Katherine said to herself, fighting for her self-control.

"Katherine, my Katy, we must talk. I—"

"Lord Milford, please don't—"

"I must, Katherine. I can't go on with this senseless

charade. Seeing you everyday, having to block you out when I want you so much."

"Sir, you are betrothed to my sister. . . ." Somehow she had managed to control her voice, keeping it cool, even cold.

From somewhere she heard a soft groan. Her hand was free and Lord Milford was standing. "You must be tired, Miss Tarkington." His voice was distant, formal.

As if in a dream she accepted his assistance in rising from the table and strolled from the salon at his side. She was only barely aware of crossing the hall, of stopping at the foot of the staircase, of watching the butler hand his lordship his hat and cane. She was only conscious of the stirring emotions within her and the burning passion she had seen in his eyes.

Katherine hadn't realized that the butler had departed. She only saw his lordship glance once more at her and then slowly, steadily, advance toward her. It wasn't happening. But there he was standing now before her.

"Katy, Katy, my dearest," she heard him whisper.

She offered no resistance when his finger, tucked gently under her chin, raised her face toward his. Suddenly the gentleness was gone. His hands were on her shoulders pulling her toward him. She felt his lips on hers, searing and demanding, his arms slipping to her waist, crushing her to him. She relaxed against him, reveling in the hardness of his body, the strength of his arms around her, lost in a world of emotional ecstacy.

Then, rising above the pounding of her blood, came the sound of Gwen's sweet laughter. Thoughts of her gentle, smiling face intruded between them.

"It's too late, milord." Katherine choked back the sobs that threatened as she tried to pull away from him.

"I'm not going to let you go, now that I know you—" His whisper was hoarse in her ear.

Steeling herself, Katherine looked at him. "Milord, if you ever cause Gwen one iota of grief, I will never speak to you again." Breaking away from him, she raced up the stairs, fighting the urge to return to him, to hang on to him.

She heard him say, "As you wish, Miss Tarkington." She felt utter despair.

Once in her room Katherine abandoned herself to an unaccustomed indulgence in tears of self-pity, aware only of the searing pain in her heart. He loved her—he loved her! And she had denied him.

Mechanically she prepared for bed—to sleep, to find oblivion. Once there she tossed and turned. Unable to find escape in sleep, she paced the room, recalling over and over again every nuance of Lord Milford's voice, his expression, his touch, until finally, she fell exhausted on the bed. The first lights of dawn were fingering their way over the horizon when she at last found the peace of sleep.

Sissy brought her hot chocolate some hours later, excited over the high success of the previous evening's ball, and eager to discuss it with her mistress. But Katherine was barely able to respond. She felt drained, depressed, devoid of the energy needed to face the ordeals of the coming day.

"Take it away, Sissy. I don't want any chocolate this morning," she commanded irritably.

"Yes, ma'am," Sissy responded meekly, her enthusiasm sharply deflated by her mistress's unwillingness to respond in kind.

"I'm sorry. I didn't mean to bark at you. I'm not feeling too pert yet. Why don't you bring me some coffee instead."

"Yes, ma'am. Right away." Sissy hurried to do her mistress's bidding.

Katherine hadn't moved when she heard the door being quietly opened.

"Your coffee, Miss Katy."

"Oh, Betsy, it's you. Thank you."

"Sissy said you weren't feeling well, so I came up to see what's the matter."

"Nothing's the matter. I'm just tired . . . so tired."

"Fiddle. I've seen you work to the wee hours of the morning, night after night, and still beat the chickens up each morning." As she spoke Betsy set the tray on the small table by Katherine's bed, her sharp eyes carefully studying the inert form huddled under the light covers. Her expression clearly showed that she was worried about what she saw.

"Maybe it's just city life," Katherine muttered despondently.

"There's more to it than that, I'm sure."

Katherine languidly stretched her arms, pulled herself to a sitting position, and then groped for the coffee cup.

"Here, Miss Katy, let me help you," Betsy offered sympathetically.

"Betsy, I don't need any help," Katherine replied fretfully as she jerked the cup, spilling the steaming coffee over her hand.

"Ohhh, look what I've done now."

Immediately Betsy was at her side, and taking the cup from her hand, she wiped the spilled coffee from her hand with her apron.

"You're not yourself, Miss Katy. Can't I help you?"

Such was the tone of Betsy's voice, expressing all the love and concern she felt for her charge that Katherine could no longer hold herself in check. The tears rolled down her cheeks and her voice broke as she sobbed. "There's nothing I—anyone—can do . . . nothing . . . nothing."

Betsy enclosed the trembling Katherine in her arms just as she had done many times in her childhood years when she had come crying to her with a scraped knee or a cut finger.

"Tell me, love, tell me. . . ."

The strain of weeks of exerting her self-control to its limits had taken its toll and Katherine could no longer endure her pain alone.

"It's Lord Milford . . . he loves me. He told me so. . . ." She stammered between her sobs. "And, Betsy, I love him so . . . with all my heart, my being, I love him."

"Ohhh, my poor darling," Betsy's voice quivered with shared grief.

Neither heard the door as it was gently closed.

Chapter XVII

Betsy relayed her mistress's excuse—the megrims—to the others that day, but by the following morning Katherine had regained her composure. Her life was not over; she would just have to endure. Lord Milford and Gwen were to be married in just a few days and she must take her expected place as sister to the bride.

A more restrained Katherine went about the remaining tasks connected with a large formal wedding. But amidst the hubbub and excitement of the preparations, the slight change in her usual calm demeanor passed unnoticed. Lady Metcalf, now fully fit, was in her glory and had seen to the catering, the decorating, the preparations necessary for the comfort of their guests. Practically everything was in readiness. Only the last minute details that always seemed to crop up were left to be taken care of at the proper time.

Two mornings before the wedding day Katherine received a letter from her steward and retired to the morning room to answer it immediately. Chewing gingerly on the tip of her pen, she was deep in thought when there was a sharp knock at the door.

"Come in," she called out distractedly.

A clearing of the throat turned her attention to the figure who had just entered.

"What is it, Reynolds?"

"Miss Janet Fairly requests permission to speak with you, milady."

"Miss Janet Fairly," Katherine repeated, perplexed. "Are you sure? She is Gwen's friend. She probably—"

"No, milady. She definitely asked for you."

Katherine frowned. *Why should she wish to speak to me?* she questioned herself. *We've hardly exchanged two words. Maybe she wants to do something special for Gwen. Yes, that must be it. . . .*

To the butler she said, "Show her to the—no, ask her to come up here, please."

"Very good, milady."

Katherine returned to the letter she had been writing and scribbled a few more words. She was signing her name when a small dark young lady burst angrily into the room.

"How could you, Miss Tarkington? How could you be so heartless?"

Startled not only by her words, but by her irate, accusing tone, Katherine could only stare at the decidedly agitated young girl who stood before her, her eyes flashing condemnation.

"Gwen has always said how wonderful you were . . . how kind and good. How could you do this . . . to her?" Her voice trembled with emotion.

"Miss Fairly, just what are you talking about?" Katherine questioned soothingly.

"Gwen . . . that's whom I'm talking about. She's going to elope with Lord Leatherton so you can have Lord Milford."

"No, no, Miss Fairly . . . you're mistaken. You must be. I don't understand." Katherine's mind was in a whirl. Gwen. Lord Leatherton. "Please, Miss Fairly, Gwen is to be married the day after tomorrow to Lord Milford. Everything is ready. Surely you've misconstrued—"

"No, I haven't. I just received this." Miss Fairly thrust a folded piece of blue stationery toward Katherine.

Katherine accepted the paper, unfolded it with shaking fingers, and read:

My dearest friend,

I have to tell someone! You are the only real friend I have now. My heart is broken! But I can't deny my sister her happiness. She has done so much for me that I must step aside for her.

I learned that she is in love with Lord Milford, and he with her. I have suspected for some time that he did not return my affection, but I felt certain that in time I could bring him around. That was before I found that his heart had already been given—to Katherine.

She doesn't know that I have discovered her secret. She would never allow me to sacrifice (that's the way she would consider my actions) myself for her.

Lord Leatherton has been the answer. He has been pursuing me assiduously, so I accepted him. I can't face Katherine or Lord Milford, so we are going to elope. I'm to meet Lord Leatherton at an inn in Thraxton—on the road to Grantham—where we will be married by special license, and then travel on to his estate at Bannington. I don't know the exact details; he's to let me know.

It's the only answer. If I just cried off, Katy would have to know the reason. I can't lie to her, she knows me too well. Once I am married to Francis, they will both be free to find their deserved happiness. I love them both so much.

I could not do this without letting you know what was in my heart, dearest friend. Think kindly of me, and may you have all the joy you merit in your forthcoming union.

Please do remember me.

With love,
Gwen

As Katherine read the carefully written letter tears welled into her eyes and slipped unhindered down her cheeks. "Oh, no . . . no . . ." she moaned as she let the missive fall unseen on the desk. "The poor sweet darling."

As Miss Fairly watched Katherine read the message, her anger seemed to die. "What are we going to do? Gwen may never speak to me again for bringing that letter to you, but I just had to. I couldn't let her run off like that . . . I just couldn't."

"You did right, Miss Fairly. Thank you for bringing this to me." She picked up the letter and handed it back to the young woman. "Right at this moment, I can't think . . . I'm too confused. I don't know where Gwen came up with these notions, but I'll do all I can to straighten things out. Thank you again. I truly appreciate what you've done."

"Gwen says you can do anything you put your mind to. I hope she's right," Miss Fairly remarked. Now there was no anger in her voice, just concern for her friend.

"I sincerely hope so," Katherine replied, as much to herself as to her companion.

Throughout the day Katherine struggled with one idea after another—none being acceptable. Not until after tea did the opportunity to formulate a plan occur.

Katherine was returning to her room and about to ascend the stairs when she heard the knocker at the door. It was rather a timid knock and did not rouse the servants, so Katherine took it upon herself to answer the door. She opened it and saw before her a ragged little urchin who looked as if he wished to be somewhere else.

"What can I do for you?" she asked him gently, so as not to send him flying on his way.

"Got a letter for Miss Tark'nton," he muttered.

"I'm Miss Tarkington."

"You sure?" he questioned, seeming to find some courage and looking at her with doubt.

"I'm sure. I've been Miss Tarkington for quite a few years."

"You look to be the right 'un. Here." He handed her the envelope he had been clutching tightly in his dirty hands, and before Katherine could thank him, he had turned and run down the steps and was out of sight within a few seconds.

Laughing, Katherine closed the door and looked curiously at the envelope. It was addressed to Miss Gwen Tarkington. She'd take it to her, as Gwen was still in the sewing room having a few last minute alterations made on her traveling gown.

Katherine continued up the stairs when the unusual

circumstances of the delivery of the letter began to bother her. Who would be writing to Gwen? She saw all her friends every day. Who would send a message by special carrier—particularly one so exceptional? Only one answer came to her. Katherine sped to her own room. Once there she opened the letter with trembling fingers, muttering as she tore the sheet slightly while pulling it from the envelope. She saw the strong, bold handwriting, and her heart sank.

> My petite,
> Tonight at 8:30 there will be a carriage waiting for you just around the corner. Nothing will keep us apart now, my little love.
>
> Yours forever,
> F.L.

Refusing to believe the words she saw, Katherine reread the brief note again. Never, never would she let Gwen marry Leatherton! But what should she do? Join her in the sewing room and forbid her to meet the carriage. What good would that do? She'd see Leatherton at Lady Beaufort's ball tonight. She couldn't watch her every second of the time. She couldn't forbid her to attend without exposing her knowledge of her sister's planned indiscretion.

Katherine paced the floor restlessly, crumbling Leatherton's note absentmindedly and stuffing it in the copious pockets of her morning dress. She knew Gwen well; complacent and pliable as she seemed to be most of the time, her sister, too, had a stubborn streak—like all the Tarkingtons, like their mother, when she had been warned not to wed an almost penniless second son, like their father, who against all odds and the knowledgeable advice of others had struggled to transform Blue Hills from a rundown drag on the pocket to the beautiful estate they now called home. If Gwen had convinced herself that she was doing the right thing, no one would be able to persuade her, bully her, or threaten her to change her mind.

There was only one course for her to take—pretend she knew nothing and at eight thirty step into that waiting carriage. She, herself, would meet Lord Leatherton. There would be no elopement. There would be no time or opportunity to arrange another—no matter how clever they were.

The matter settled, Katherine immediately proceeded to detail her plans. She would have to take a valise and at least one bandbox. The driver would expect some luggage—not much. Quickly she packed a few things, not caring what she brought, as she would not be using them, and hid the two pieces of luggage in the back of the closet. Satisfied with her initial step, she considered her next. But there was nothing else to do—not until eight thirty.

The time seemed to drag by for Katherine, but finally they had finished an early, informal dinner and retired to their own rooms to ready themselves for the last festive event before Gwen's wedding. As Lady Metcalf was a close friend of Lady Beaufort's, she, too, was attending the affair, and the three ladies were going in her coach, Lord Milford and Philip to meet them there.

Fortunately Sissy had expressed a desire to attend a performance of the circus with a number of her friends, so it had been a simple matter of dismissing her for the evening. When Katherine entered her room, her gown for the evening had been laid out, but the room was empty. Instead of putting on the elaborate ball gown awaiting her, Katherine hurriedly donned a dark traveling dress from her wardrobe.

Then she pulled the valise and bandbox from their hiding place, slipped on a hooded cape, and moved toward the door. No one would be looking for her for at least an hour. What then? Katherine dropped her luggage and hurried to her desk. She took a piece of paper and a pen and scribbled a few words, crossed them out, tore up the paper, and grabbed another sheet. She wrote:

> Dear Betsy,
>
> Make my apologies to Gwen and Lady Metcalf. I just couldn't bring myself to attend the ball tonight. Say that it is my wish that they proceed with their plans for this evening. I'll explain tomorrow.
>
> Love,
> Katy

There, she thought, that didn't say too much. By the time they found this note, it would be too late. Their only recourse would be to follow her instructions. Katherine propped the note up on her dresser, and without a backward glance quietly opened the door, stealthily stepped into the hall, and left the house.

By the time Katherine turned the corner, darkness had fallen, but she could still make out a carriage standing a few hundred feet away. Not hesitating a second, she marched up to it. At her approach the driver jumped to the ground, touched his cap respect-fully, and took her valise and bandbox, stowing them on the seat next to him. Then he let down the steps and assisted her to climb into the coach. Not one word was exchanged.

Katherine decided that this was a hired coach. Though it was comfortable enough, it was not ornate or sufficiently luxurious to carry the Leatherton label, though she suspected the driver was Leatherton's man. He seemed to know exactly what to do.

Having no idea how long it would take them to ar-rive at the inn in Thraxton, or even where Thraxton was, Katherine made herself comfortable. But she could not relax. She didn't want to think, she didn't want to feel. If only she could clear her mind, make it a complete blank. That was impossible. Instead her thoughts drifted back over the past months. Should she have done anything differently? Should she never have gone to Milford Hall in the first place? There would have been no night at Charity's, no Miss Bot-tomsly. The thought left her empty. No, she would never want to give up those memories. Katherine could not bring herself to feel guilty about her love for Lord Milford. No, that was a wonderful, true emo-tion, and she could attach no wrong to it. Her only remorse lay in the pain and agitation that she knew Gwen must be experiencing through no fault of her own. Sweet Gwen! She would have her Lord Milford and Milford Hall too.

The rocking motion of the coach and the relief brought by the undertaking of a definite plan of ac-tion, added to a real deficit of sleep, soon were too much for Katherine to resist, and she dozed.

The halt of the coach awakened her. She looked at the small lapel watch pinned to her dress, but it was now too dark to see the tiny hands. Glancing out the window, she discovered that they had pulled into the dimly lit court of an old-fashioned inn—The Dancing Horse. What an unusual name, she thought. The huge hanging sign depicted a beautiful black stallion reared up on its hind legs, pawing the air.

The driver set down the steps for her descent. As Katherine scanned the scene around her she could see no other lights, no evidence of any other buildings. Evidently Thraxton was not a very large village or the inn was situated outside its perimeter. She accepted the driver's assistance and followed him into the building. Her luggage held easily under his arm, he spoke quietly to a fleshy, older man who had immediately greeted them at the entrance as if he had been lying in wait. The innkeeper, or so Katherine surmised, nodded his head, his thick jowls quivering from the exertion. His heavily lidded eyes blinked at her for a few seconds before he impassively indicated that she was to follow him.

Katherine was uneasy—not afraid, but wary. She did not like finding herself in a situation in which she had no control, nor knew exactly what was going to happen next. Yet there was nothing she could do now but follow the innkeeper's direction. He led her into a very pleasant parlor, small, but well equipped, clean, and inviting.

"You're to await his lordship here, miss. My missus will be bringing some refreshments shortly." His voice was civil, neither friendly nor unfriendly. He was just following instructions.

Chapter XVIII

Gwen tapped lightly on Katy's door.

"Are you ready? It's nine thirty. Should I send Betsy to assist you?"

There was no answer.

Frowning, Gwen tapped louder. "Katy, Katy dear." She had raised her voice, but still received no response.

Puzzled, Gwen pushed open the door and peered inside. Candles flickered in the draft, but their intermittent light showed no evidence of the room's occupancy. Gwen stepped in. "Katy, where are you hiding? What are you up to?"

She spied Katherine's ball gown spread out on the bed and the morning dress she had been wearing that day lying rumpled beside it. "Katy!" Her voice was almost a scream.

Running into the hall, Gwen called repeatedly, "Katy, Katy." Then she changed the name to Betsy. In a second the old servant came scurrying in response.

"What is it, Miss Gwen? What's the matter?" she questioned breathlessly, taking the agitated girl gently by the arm.

"Katy's gone—she's not in her room—her gown is

still on the bed." Gwen's words tumbled out fearfully.

Betsy rushed into Katherine's room to see in a glance that all Gwen had said was true. Stunned, Betsy stared at the ball gown, the tiny jewels sewn into the bodice unconcernedly reflecting the glow of the firelight. As if in a daze, and from long years of habit, she picked up the morning dress Katherine had discarded. As she folded it carefully over her arm, she saw the note on the dressing table.

"Miss Gwen, she's left a note." There was some relief in her voice.

Quickly Gwen picked up the folded piece of paper, then, puzzled, she handed it unread to Betsy. "It's addressed to you."

As if suspecting something of its contents, Betsy accepted it reluctantly and read the few words.

"Oh, my poor darling." A moan escaped her compressed lips.

"What's the matter, Betsy? Tell me!" an almost frantic Gwen pleaded with her.

"Miss Katy's all right, Miss Gwen . . . it's just she—she didn't feel up to another ball tonight and couldn't think of a good excuse . . ." Betsy improvised lamely.

"That's not true. You're hiding something from me." Impatiently Gwen took the note from Betsy, but its brief contents told her no more. But there was no need. Gwen knew the reason—she knew why Katherine could not attend Lady Beaufort's ball, why she could not face Lord Milford the last night before his wedding.

Slowly Gwen walked over to the bed and, fingering the beautiful gown, murmured absently, "She should have gone, Betsy. Lord Milford would have loved her even more in this dress." Tears were slowly rolling down her cheeks.

"You know?"

"Yes, I know, Betsy. I've known for some time. I heard her confiding in you that morning. I wasn't eavesdropping—it was just bad timing, I guess." Gwen smiled weakly as Betsy's face registered her ever deepening sympathy.

"But everything is going to be all right, Betsy," Gwen continued briskly as she wiped away the tears. "I'm not going to marry Lord Milford."

"But . . . but—"

"I've worked everything out." So saying, Gwen embraced the old servant warmly. As she did so there was the sound of crackling paper between them. Automatically Betsy's hand searched for the pockets of Katherine's dress that she still held folded over her arm.

"Miss Katy's always cluttering up her pockets with odd bits of paper. I wonder if this is of any importance." She pulled out Lord Leatherton's note and proceeded to smooth the crumbled sheet of paper.

Catching sight of the bold F. L. signature, Gwen gasped and snatched the missive from her hands. Hurriedly, breathlessly, she read the boldly written words. A numbness came over her, and she slipped listlessly down on the bed, dropping the note on the floor.

"No, no, she didn't," Gwen whispered huskily.

Betsy, confused and worried, hastily picked up the missive, and she, too, read it. But it meant nothing to her.

"Eight thirty tonight. . . . What does this mean, Miss Gwen?"

"It means, it means," Gwen stammered, "that Katherine's discovered my plans and is trying to upset them."

As she spoke she seemed to gain resolve. "Well, she's not going to do it!"

With that remark Gwen jumped up from the bed and turned to the old servant. "I'm going to marry Lord Leatherton tonight, and that's that."

Gwen rushed out of the room, a frightened, pleading Betsy coming after her. Entering her own room, Gwen took out a pelisse and drew it around her shoulders over her gown. There was no time to change. In any case the delightful creation she was wearing would make a splendid wedding dress. She pulled a silk scarf from her drawer and hastily tied it around her head. All the while Betsy was demanding to be told what she was about, but Gwen continued to ignore her. She picked up her reticule, tossed a few pieces of jewelry that were lying on her dressing table into it, and then, after a brief look around the room, started for the door.

Betsy was quicker. She planted herself in Gwen's path, and with the voice she had so often used to discipline the younger Tarkingtons, she said, "You're not going anyplace, young lady. Not, at least, until you tell me what this is all about."

"There's no time now, Betsy. Please."

But the servant did not move, her face stern with disapproval.

In exasperation Gwen blurted out, "I've made plans to meet Lord Leatherton at The Dancing Horse in Thraxton, where we are to be married. I'm sure that's where Katy has gone. She's going to force me to marry

Lord Milford, and I won't have it that way . . . I won't, I won't. Katherine can't stop me. You can't stop me either." Abruptly she changed her defiant tone to one of pleading. "Please, Betsy, it's best my way."

Gwen could sense that Betsy was weakening and quickly took advantage of her indecision to dart around her and out the door. She raced to the servants' stairs. Without slowing she sped down them, out into the courtyard, and across to the stables.

"Sommers, Sommers, I need you immediately," she called, a rising note of hysteria in her voice.

"What is it, missy?"

"There's no time to explain. Miss Katy's in danger. We have to get to Thraxton in a hurry," she lied expediently.

Blinking, the elderly man just looked at her.

Using every bit of wit and guile at her command, Gwen soon had Sommers and the young stableboy harnessing up the horses to the coach with all the speed they could muster.

Betsy had again joined Gwen, begging her to reconsider, commanding her to forgo her foolish flight. But Gwen was adamant. All the old servant could do was stand by helplessly with an openmouthed stableboy and watch the carriage rumble out of the yard.

"Where's Thraxton?" A young voice brought Betsy to her senses.

"Don't you know?"

"Nope. Neither does Mr. Sommers," replied the mystified youth.

"Oh, what a fiasco!" exclaimed Betsy. Then, turning to the lad, she asked, "Do you know where Lady Beaufort's place is?"

"Oh, sure, everyone knows that. 'Tis 'bout half mile down the road," he answered, feeling important.

Relieved that it was fairly close, Betsy continued, "You hurry over there and find Lord Milford. Tell him, and him only, that there's trouble here and he's needed. Can you do that?"

"S'pose so."

"There'll be a couple of shillings for you when you get back, and I'll tell Cook to give you tarts for dessert every night next week."

"Lady Beaufort's . . . Lord Milford . . . trouble . . . needed here," the lad repeated, and after a quick nod from Betsy, he left, his bare feet slapping on the cobblestones as he ran out the courtyard into the street.

Betsy murmured a silent prayer, and returned to the house, racking her brain for the best explanation she could devise to give Lady Metcalf for the scandalous behavior of her two young mistresses.

Lord Milford and Philip conversed amiably as they stood near the entrance, obviously awaiting the arrival of some particular guests of Lady Beaufort. Already the ballroom and salons were crowded with ladies exquisitely gowned and with elegant gentlemen paying them court. The once crowded entrance hall was thinning out, and the butler had no difficulty in finding Lord Milford.

"Milord," the butler addressed him respectfully, "one of Lady Metcalf's stableboys says he has an urgent message for you."

Quizzically his lordship repeated, "One of Lady Metcalf's stableboys?"

"Yes, little Ronnie. Our groom knows him well."

He's known—then this is no prank, thought Lord Milford, remembering the last urgent message he had received. Frowning, he turned to Philip. "Wonder what this is all about. Coming with me?"

"Of course," Philip answered without hesitating.

The butler led the two gentlemen down the hall to a small pantrylike room far removed from the flow of party guests. There the lad stood, restlessly awaiting them.

"Well," Lord Milford greeted him, "you have a message for me."

"Yes, milord." The stableboy recognized him immediately, having taken his magnificent great bay from his lordship many a time during the past few months. "Miss Hatfield told me to tell you that there was trouble and that you were needed."

"Trouble? What kind of trouble?" Concern made his lordship's voice harsh.

"I dunno! All I knows is that Miss Tark'nton comes runnin' out the house and gets me and Mr. Sommers to hitch up the carriage. They're off to Thraxton."

"Thraxton?"

"Yes, milord." The lad's head bobbed up and down, accenting his confirmation.

Lord Milford gave Philip a quick troubled look. "Let's go." Tossing the boy a coin, he turned and strode out of the room, Philip right behind him.

Neither had noticed that while the butler had been speaking with Lord Milford, Lord Leatherton had been hovering in the vicinity. They did not see the sardonic smile that had curved his lips—nor the triumphant gleam that brightened his eyes as the two followed the butler from the ballroom. Neither did they know of his immediate departure, his great black stallion being held ready for instant flight.

Upon arriving at Lady Metcalf's, Lord Milford and Philip encountered an agitated Miss Hatfield, worried about her mistresses, yet with her self-control intact.

She explained the situation to them quickly and concisely, having already prepared her tale. Unsure how the sisters would have wanted her to handle the matter, she only told them that Miss Katy had left for The Dancing Horse in Thraxton to meet Lord Leatherton at about eight thirty and that Miss Gwen had followed after her at about ten o'clock. As to why, she couldn't say. But she did add that she was uneasy about the whole affair and thought it best to tell them. Possibly they would know what to do.

Lord Milford readily perceived that Miss Hatfield had glossed over many details in her revelation of the events of that evening and that she was more than uneasy about her mistresses. In addition he knew Lord Leatherton! He realized that he would gain no more information from the old servant.

Concealing his own anguish, his lordship reassured Miss Hatfield, and the two gentlemen were soon again astride their mounts, racing toward the Grantham road.

Katherine sipped the refreshing hot tea, thankful for its reviving effect, but she could not force herself to partake of any of the delicate tarts that had been placed before her.

How long was she to wait for Lord Leatherton? How would he react to her presence? she wondered

208

and smiled faintly as she contemplated his chagrin. She did, however, feel a moment's pang of sympathy for the poor priest that Leatherton would be dragging along with him. Well, anyway, she reflected, he would have a pleasant evening for his journey.

She had seated herself in a comfortable high-back chair facing the small but adequate fireplace and was gazing at the feeble flames poking in and out of the stacked logs, diverted as usual by thoughts of another night in another country inn, when she heard the sound of a horse's hoofs, which ceased in front of the inn. Shortly thereafter the door to the parlor was flung open and the soft, purring voice of Lord Leatherton greeted her.

"My petite, you are truly here." The high back of the chair had hidden her real identity.

With a few strides he was beside her, and then before her. The instant he saw Katherine, the lights in his eyes turned to angry flames, his pleasant smile became distorted in rage. "You! What are you doing here?"

Katherine calmly raised her eyes to his. Just the expression she had pictured, she thought. She shuddered, but her voice was firm and cold. "I am here, Lord Leatherton, to stop a very inadvisable wedding to which my sister was to have been a part."

Katherine watched him, fascinated, as he fought for control. His initial surprise had erupted immediately into fury. Slowly the murderous passion subsided, and as he returned her stare a malicious sneer curved his lips. Suddenly he threw back his head and burst into ominous laughter completely devoid of mirth that set Katherine's every nerve to tingling.

"Wedding, my dear Miss Tarkington. Don't tell me you are as foolish as your little sister."

Horror filled her eyes. "You mean there was to be no marriage?"

"Marry a silly little chit like her? Really, what do you take me for?"

Now, in turn, rage stirred within Katherine. "You never meant to marry her. You were going to drag her name through the mud to satisfy your own greed and need for vengeance!"

Contemptuously he snorted, "You might conclude something like that."

"Thank God I came," Katherine murmured as she closed her eyes and leaned back in her chair, unable to look at the loathsome human being before her.

"You won't be thanking God or anyone when this evening is over," he whispered menacingly. Lord Leatherton had stepped closer and bent over her until his face was only a few inches from her own.

Katherine opened her eyes and pressed back harder against the chair, chilled by the icy anger in the dark eyes so near her own. "You came to save your sister—who will come to save you?" He straightened up and chuckled maliciously. "I might be denied my vengeance tonight, but I'll not be denied my pleasure."

"You wouldn't dare!" Katherine spat at him fiercely.

"Oh, wouldn't I? You came here unattended—of your own free will. Who's to blame me?"

"You are despicable."

"But with so much more *savoir vivre* than that shadow of Milford's that's been dangling after you," he crooned insolently.

"You're not half the man either one of them is," Katherine snapped back, her eyes blazing in anger.

"Ohhh, I like that, I like that. Fire and spirit. But we're wasting time here." With that he grasped her arm and raised her from her chair. Katherine resisted with all her strength, striking at the arm that held her in a grip of steel.

"Not yet, not yet, my firy vixen. Not here. I like a more compatible setting. Here, slip on your cape." He took the garment from the back of a nearby chair and threw it around her shoulders.

"No, no, leave the hood down. If anyone should see us, I want him to get a good look at my beauteous prize."

Fear intermingled with fury as Katherine faced him and hissed, "Take your hand off me or I'll scream until the very devil quakes."

Lord Leatherton roared in appreciative laughter. "Go ahead, scream away. Surprising how deaf money makes some people." He jerked her arm behind her and propelled her toward the door.

Unable to combat his superior strength, Katherine staggered in the direction she was pushed. Her pride asserted itself and she regained her poise, walking down the hall, her head high, her eyes blazing.

The same carriage that had brought Katherine to the inn was waiting by the entrance, the driver impassively seated with the reins in hand, ready to spring the horses forward. Leatherton easily lifted Katherine into the coach and with a graceful leap was instantly seated beside her. The carriage lunged and moved rapidly out of the courtyard onto the road.

Katherine sought hurriedly for a plan of escape. Where were they? Where were they going? What was Leatherton going to do? She laughed bitterly to herself. She knew just what he intended. She would fight to the death before she would let him lay a hand on her.

Lord Leatherton was quiet as they moved swiftly and smoothly along the road, but when the coach made a sharp turn and the road became rough, jostling the carriage every which way, he gently steadied her.

"Not much longer now," he informed her, his voice susurrant, almost apologetic. Again he appeared to be the same obliging gentlemen the sisters had come to know.

Peering out the windows, Katherine beheld only blackness. Lost in her own frightened, angered turmoil of emotions, she had no idea how much time had elapsed before the carriage slowed to a halt.

"My lodge, my dear." Leatherton grasped her hand, and then jumped nimbly to the ground, still maintaining his grip. He pulled her forward. "Wouldn't want you to get lost in these woods." His grip tightened as Katherine tried to pull away.

As Katherine's feet touched the ground she again struggled to free herself. "Now don't be tiresome, my feisty one. I won't let you go . . . not yet!" With that he picked her up bodily and carried her toward the lights that blinked in the solid blackness of the building before them.

Realizing her helplessness at the moment, Katherine chose to conserve her strength for a more opportune time. Lord Leatherton was a big man, almost as tall as Lord Milford, and there was no denying his strength. But somehow she would find a way.

He carried her up two steps, and then kicked at the door, which was immediately opened by a thin, haggard-looking man whose small, watery eyes saw no one's troubles but his own.

There would be no assistance here, Katherine realized.

"Is everything prepared, Thomas?"

"As you've ordered, sir." A thin, quivering voice answered him.

"Then go. I don't want to see you again tonight," Leatherton commanded sharply.

"Yes, milord." And he was gone.

Still carrying Katherine, Lord Leatherton entered the main room of the lodge. There he set her down on her feet and gently removed her cape. Startled, Katherine gasped in amazement. Under other circumstances she would have loved this spacious, luxurious room. A huge stone fireplace dominated the end wall, the soft glow of the embers lighting up the large fur rug spread on the floor before it. One side wall was lined with shelves of books; two large, richly upholstered divans were placed strategically in the center while comfortable chairs and a conveniently placed table were interspersed throughout. The other wall—Katherine guessed it to be the front of the house—was taken up with a row of long narrow mullioned windows flanked by the heavy folds of dark burgundy drapes, which Leatherton proceeded to close as Katherine was surveying her surroundings.

"Cozier this way," he said softly, his eyes glinting malevolently. "I thought you'd find this a more pleasant setting."

"A lovely room," Katherine agreed coolly.

Leatherton chuckled. "A little wine, my dear?"

What kind of cat and mouse game was he playing, Katherine asked herself and realized she had chosen a very apt simile. He was the cat and she was the mouse!

"It would be a shame to waste this champagne," he urged.

"Why all this"—Katherine swept her arm around the room—"if you weren't planning a marriage?"

"Oh, a little whimsy of mine." He paused, another sardonic smile crossing his face. "I just wondered how long it would take 'til sweet little Gwen caught on."

Katherine bit her lip to quell her revulsion. He seemed willing to talk. Maybe if she kept him talking she could persuade him . . . now that his first flare of temper had died down.

"Champagne? Yes, I'll have a glass."

"That's better." He filled two glasses and brought one to Katherine who had taken a seat in one of the chairs near the fireplace.

Automatically she thanked him and, after taking a few sips, turned an earnest face toward him. "But why? Why this whole affair . . . with Gwen? I understand you dislike Lord Milford, but this elaborate—"

"Why, you ask?" Lord Leatherton interrupted as he took a position by the fireplace, casually resting his arm on the mantel. "I'll tell you why. It's a long story, covers three generations, but I'll make it brief." He paused to take a sip of his wine. "Years ago Milford's grandfather cheated mine out of his lands, his wealth, and even his life. My father swore he'd get it all back, and together we almost did. Only one estate remained to be retrieved—the finest of them all, Milford Hall. My father died before he was able to complete his design, but I'm determined to finish it." There was bitterness and hatred in every word he spoke: a calmness, a calculating coldness that frightened Katherine even more than did his rage.

"But you have so much already. You don't really need—"

"You don't understand, my dear. It's not a matter of need in the material sense. It's a matter of solace for one's pride. My father took care of old Lord Milford and his grandson Jonathan—the devil and his protégé. Fate took care of the devil's weakling cub. It's my place to put an end to the task." As he spoke Katherine could sense his grimness, his complete obsession.

"I understood Milford's grandfather and brother were killed in a racing accident," Katherine interposed, saying whatever came to mind just to keep him talking.

"Why, of course, it was a racing accident, my dear." Again his voice was silky, soft. "But who do you imagine instigated the bet? Who do you imagine picked the terrain for the race? Who do you imagine saw to it that a wheel was loose?"

"Diabolical!" Katherine murmured.

"True, diabolically clever. No one ever suspected. Even if someone had, there would be no way of proving a thing."

Leatherton had moved over to her chair and seated

himself on its arm, letting his hand move idly, gently over Katherine's shoulder.

Repressing a shudder, Katherine attempted to pull away from him. Leatherton uttered a soft chuckle and continued his tender caress.

"But what did you expect to gain by ruining my sister's reputation?"

"I must admit my plan was not as satisfactory as my father's. Then again, Milford and I don't travel in the same circle and I was having a devilishly difficult time keeping tabs on him. This little sortie was just a stopgap. You understand, dear Katherine." His hand now gripped her shoulder firmly. "There must not be another heir to contend with, so there must not be a marriage. The right honorable Earl of Sandwell would hardly marry secondhand merchandise."

Katherine groaned. She felt sick. "Maybe he would never know," she muttered weakly.

Again Leatherton laughed. Katherine's stomach turned over. "Don't give that a thought. I took care of every detail," he continued, seemingly delighted to display his cleverness. "Someone conveniently informed him of part of my plans. Why, he even left Lady Beaufort's before I did. I imagine that he is now racing to Bannington to rescue his errant bride."

He broke his story with a satanic chuckle. "There he'll be informed of the existence of his lodge. I expect him here sometime in the early morning."

"But he won't find Gwen . . ." Katherine moaned.

Leatherton smiled sweetly at her. "No, he won't, but by that time the wedding will have had to be postponed—time to devise another plan."

Katherine had not heard the finish of his statement. Her only thoughts were of the possibility—no, no, no! Horror, humiliation, fear, loathing—all these emotions played across her face as she stared wide-eyed at this composed, handsome young man at her side.

"My dear, you're vexed with me. No need to be. If you so wish, we can be gone before he arrives."

Katherine gasped her relief. "Then, you've changed your—"

Leatherton leaned closer. "Not a chance. As delightful as your sister might have been, you are so much more desirable, so much more of a woman."

Breathing heavily, he rose and pulled her from the chair. Frantically Katherine twisted from his grasp, only to be caught again. He pulled her to him, pressed his lips savagely on hers.

"There, there it is," yelled Philip. "To your right."

Lord Milford glanced in that direction and was able to make out the wide dirt trail that turned off from the main road. He guided his horse on to it, slowing the pace because of the uneven ruts and furrows.

Philip, now riding at his side, spoke up. "It will be slower going for this stretch, but in the long run it will save time. Our horses can catch their second wind."

"You know the territory better than I, Philip," Milford answered tersely as his anxiety mounted with the passing of each second.

They rode silently for some time, each lost in his own thoughts. Then Philip heard him mutter, "Why did she do it? Why?"

"It's obvious, Gerry," Philip consoled. "She was just

trying to keep Katherine from running off with Leatherton. Though I can't understand why Katherine would."

"Fool!" Gerald almost shouted. "Katherine would never run off with Leatherton."

Shocked by the unexpected vehemence of Milford's statement, Philip remained silent.

"She loves me and she knew how much I loved her. Leatherton—"

"Just what do you mean—you love Katherine? You're marrying Gwen!" Anger was ringing in Philip's voice.

"My God, Philip, I've made a botch of everything," Milford said bitterly. "My blindness, my stupid pride! I fell in love with Katherine when I believed her to be Miss Hatfield—maybe I didn't realize it then, but even if I had, it wouldn't have made any difference. Hummp! A governess wasn't good enough for the Earl of Sandwell! I chose Gwen."

"And you called *me* a fool."

"You're right. *I'm* the fool."

"What about Gwen? Does she know?"

"Of course not," Milford answered. "Katherine forbid me to speak of it to her. In a way she was forcing me to act like an honorable man." Self-loathing filled his voice.

"Poor Gwen . . . so happy . . . so lovely." A new note of sympathy had entered Philip's voice.

Milford swore as his horse stumbled but quickly righted itself. They rode on in silence.

In time they saw the faint lights of The Dancing Horse. In minutes they pulled their mounts to a halt before its door. Both men leaped to the ground.

"You talk to the innkeeper. I'll see what they have to say in the stables," Milford commanded.

Philip nodded and entered the inn while Lord Milford made his way to the side and on to the rear where the stables stood, dark and silent.

The innkeeper greeted Philip pleasantly, his fleshy face bouncing as he bowed. Upon hearing Philip's questions, he became wary, but still civil. Yes, there had been a young woman here earlier. Yes, Lord Leatherton arrived soon after, and they rode away together in his coach. No, he didn't know where they were going—but he did hear Lord Leatherton describing Bannington, his estates near Grantham, while they were leaving.

Philip thanked him, turned, and was just about to leave when the front door was pushed open and Gwen's diminutive figure rushed in.

"Philip!" she cried in astonishment. "What are you doing here? Where's Katy?"

"I—I . . . she's gone."

"Gone? Already? Where's Lord Leatherton?" Seeing the sympathy, then the anguish in Philip's eyes, she stiffened. "Philip, what have I done?" She threw herself, sobbing, into his arms.

"There, there, Gwen. You tried. You did your best." Philip soothed her, stroked her hair gently.

"Sommers didn't know the way . . . we took so long. My best! No, Philip, no, you have it all wrong. *I* was running away with Lord Leatherton. Somehow she found out and went to put a stop to it."

"You were going to elope with Leatherton?" Philip asked her, amazement in his voice.

"Lord Milford and Katy are so much in love . . . I—I'm just in the way. I was sure that it would be best."

"You poor silly thing." He tightened his arms around her.

Unseen, Lord Milford had entered the inn and heard the whole of Gwen's tale. Brusquely he interrupted them. "Leatherton has a hunting lodge about five miles from here. You take care of Gwen." Milford whirled and was away before Philip could reply.

Driving his horse with a frenzy he had never before experienced, Lord Milford cursed, promised, and pleaded that he would be in time. The miles flew by under the steady pounding of the great bay's hoofs and Lord Milford soon saw the rosy hue of lighted windows. Abruptly pulling his horse to a halt, he dismounted and ran, quietly for such a man in such a state of mind.

He found the door unlocked and entered unhesitantly, rushing toward the sounds of scuffling feet and muffled screams. Flinging open the door to the main room, he felt his temper rage to the breaking point, seeing Leatherton and Katherine locked in a desperate struggle.

"Leatherton." His voice, cold and sharp, sliced through the sounds of their exertion.

Instantly Leatherton released his hold on Katherine, who fell unceremoniously to the floor.

"Would you care to go a round with one your own size and weight?" All the contempt he felt for Leatherton colored his icy tones.

"Not really, Gerry," Leatherton replied coolly as he

smoothed out his finely tailored coat. "Fisticuffs are so vulgar."

"Forcing your attentions on a helpless female is much more gentile!" sneered Milford.

Unruffled, Leatherton replied, "Maybe not more gentile, but the rewards are so much more satisfying. But if you'd dare to cross swords, I'd be delighted to accommodate you."

Katherine listened to the exchange in astounded relief as she pulled herself up from the rug and went to stand behind Milford.

"My pleasure, sir" was Milford's curt answer.

Dazed, and somewhat confused by what she thought was a silly dialogue, Katherine caught his lordship's arm. "He means to kill you."

"I know, my love, I know." Milford leaned over and kissed her gently. "Don't worry. I'll see to it that he doesn't."

Now thoroughly aware of what was happening, she held on to his arm. "Gerry . . . Milford . . . my dearest," Katherine cried, her heart in her eyes. All the fear she had felt for herself was now transferred to the man she loved.

Gently releasing her hand from his arm, he spoke to her softly. "Remember I love you, I'll love only you . . . always."

The two men unscathed their swords, removed their coats and shoes. Carefully they rolled up their sleeves. Lord Leatherton pushed aside a few pieces of furniture, and then turned to face Lord Milford.

"I see that you are not the fool I thought you were, Gerald. Did you plan to have both the sisters?" A sneer marred his elegant face.

"My activities before and after this meeting are none of your affair, Francis."

"You are wrong about that, but this moment is of utmost importance to me now."

They saluted and fought. Katherine watched, terrified, trembling at every feint, every lunge. The faint glow from the fire flickered off the flashing swords. Beads of perspiration glistened on their faces; soaked the fine fabric of their shirts where it was stretched across their muscular backs. A lifetime of hatred, and an ever mounting desire for vengeance spurred Leatherton on while years of active military service had honed Milford's skills. They were evenly matched. For Katherine all time ceased—the world no longer existed.

Then it was over. Leatherton lay moaning on the floor, blood oozing from a deep wound in his side. Lord Milford stood over him, glaring down at him. "I should have killed you!"

"Katy, Katy," Gwen screamed as she ran into the room, Philip close behind her.

The two sisters embraced, soothing, calming, and reassuring each other.

"What kept you so long, Philip? Take care of him." Milford jerked his head toward Leatherton, who was now unconscious. "No, he's not dead. But he soon will be if you don't stop that bleeding. I'll get his man to go for a doctor."

As if still in the fields of France, Philip jumped to attend the wounded man as his commander, Lord Milford, left the room, without looking at the two sisters locked in each other's arms.

Finally Gwen controlled her tears and broke from the embrace. "I'm all right now, Katy. I'm so sorry. I've been such a fool. I never suspected what a beast he was."

"I know, Gwen. Neither did I. We were just two naive country girls." Katherine smiled. "Everything's all right now. It's a good thing we've planned an afternoon wedding. We'll be back in plenty of time."

Gwen looked at her sister in astonishment. "You can't mean that you still want me to— No, no, there's not going to be any wedding. At least not mine!"

"But, Gwen, you—"

"Listen to me, dear sister. Just for once listen to me." Gwen stood facing her sister, fire in her eyes. "All my life you've told me what was best for me. All my life you've done everything for me, for Cliff, for Agatha. You've given up your own chances of a future for us. Well, that's all over. You're going to have your own life now. It's my turn to be good, to be noble, and you're not going to take that away from me!" Gwen glared vehemently and waited in defiance for Katherine to reply.

There was no reply. Katherine was too stunned to say a word.

Then softly Gwen continued, "Besides, Katy, how could I marry a man who was in love with someone else? That's a poor basis for a good marriage."

"She's right, you know." Lord Milford's voice whispered in her ear. He had come up silently behind Katherine and gently rested his hands on her shoulders.

Throwing Lord Milford a grateful glance, Gwen

turned away and was joined by Philip, who led her to one of the divans and gently eased her down, seating himself next to her.

Katherine and Lord Milford were no longer aware of them, for he had slowly turned her around to face him.

"Miss Hatfield," he spoke formally, "if you could persuade your mistress to marry me, I promise to give you the pleasant, but probably somewhat tiring, task of rearing our brood of children."

Katherine sighed as she leaned against him. He dropped his arms to her waist. "Miss Katherine Tarkington, would you do me the honor of becoming mistress of Milford Hall?" He kissed her gently, and her arms entwined around his neck as her eyes gave him the answer he desired.

He kissed her again, not so gently. Katherine pulled back, breathless, but still managed to ask, "What about Miss Bottomsly?"

He held her tighter, crushing her to him, as he buried his head in her hair. "Hush, I wasn't going to mention her. I want her for my mistress."